THE TREASURE OF THE SEAS

By Joseph Gaspare LoNigro

ISBN: 13: 978-0615693002
ISBN-10:0615693008

For Holly, Kolby and Troy

For Mom and Dad

Acknowledgements

Special thanks to Dr. David Danielson for being my test reader and sounding board. You will always get everything first-whether you want it or not. Also, a special thanks to my editor Maryan Pelland who pushed and mentored me in the right direction.

CHAPTER ONE

Two years ago. Arabian Sea. Off the coast of Somalia.

Abdi Dalmar's bald black head bobbed in the water like an upside down fisherman's lure. Between gasps for air, he wondered how he had gotten himself into this situation. His hands were tied behind his back — his ankles were bound with rope and tied to a large piece of wood that jutted over the side of a boat that was picking up speed by the second. Dalmar could hear men onboard the *Sea Wolf* laughing as they carried out his torturous sentence. The boat hopped through the water while his head bounced in and out of the ocean, filling his nostrils and mouth with tepid sea water. He tasted sea salt mixed with his blood each time the force of the waves lacerated his scalp. He remembered watching this process from the other side on more than a few occasions, and his mind cut to scenes of shredded faces and torsos pulled back on board after other men were tortured to death.

Today, however, would be another of those days that confirmed in Dalmar's mind that he was indeed more than lucky. He was, to his thinking, touched in some way. The wooden plank, weakened from years of stress, had snapped like a tree hit by lightning and catapulted itself into the ocean. By the time drunken crew members noticed, Dalmar was far in the Sea Wolf's wake. When he realized his good fortune, he smiled. Raising his head from the water, he vowed a bloody revenge.

Much later, not feeling any particular anxiety, Dalmar bobbed and swooshed along in the sea, letting his thoughts wander as he waited for whatever would come next. He remembered with pride, almost arrogance, when during his late teen years he was one of his country's most celebrated soccer players. He had grown to an impressive six feet four inches with long, hard legs and a tight muscular chest. In contrast to his trademark rounded bald head, a classic square jaw jutted in front of him. His internal motor kept him in constant motion evidenced by his round black eyes darting from place to place, person to person. Those eyes sent a chill down your spine when his gaze landed on you. When Dalmar walked into a room or strode onto the pitch he was totally in charge. It never mattered whether he was the most skilled player on the field, it was always clear that Dalmar was the most dominant, and that intensity never flagged, on or off the field.

Despite the fact that the Somali National team had never been to a world cup match, they had what looked like their best club in decades. The national team, nicknamed the Ocean Stars, was headed in the right direction and Dalmar gave it everything he had.

"Dalmar is perfect on defense," his coach bragged. "The guy wouldn't let a shadow get past. He's not giving anyone a piece of our goal, ever."

In every game, Dalmar put his head down, his focus on a single mission: *Nobody gets that ball by me.*

His relentlessness became legendary among his mates and dragged him into many a tussle in both practice and games. He prided himself on never having lost a fight, but his willingness to mix it up created a huge hole in his game. Opponents recognized his quick temper and took every opportunity to goad him. Penalties ultimately cost the Ocean Stars games, and that cost Dalmar a ton of playing time.

After one brief practice skirmish he head-butted a teammate, crushing the guy's nose and causing him permanent eye damage. The coach banned Dalmar from practice for a month.

Dalmar could still see the coach jabbing a fat finger at him and barking, "Now, you're gonna learn a lesson and control that damned temper?"

Dalmar did not. He spent four weeks seething, getting no closer to the action than a pair of lame binoculars and a seat on the floor of an abandoned building near the field. He took copious notes on each practice, then went home and drilled meticulously by himself. After his suspension, he swaggered back as if he'd never missed a day.

A few weeks later he tackled another teammate, tearing the player's kneecap from its socket, grotesquely turning the joint nearly one-hundred and eighty degrees. Dalmar recalled the player's shriek of agony. With the rest of the team gathered around the victim, Dalmar shrugged, puzzled by the hoopla.

"I was just doing my job. He fouled me," Dalmar said over his shoulder as he bent to adjust a shoe. He would not change his style of play for anyone, not even his teammates.

Both coaches and mates had had enough. After a long meeting they confronted Dalmar yet again. This time, the message got stronger; however, he wasn't particularly impressed with threats. The conversation didn't stand out in his memory but it went something like, "Listen Dalmar, either you dial it down, at least during practice, or we're through with you. You're gone."

Dalmar had a vague memory of considering this ultimatum and then discarding it as nonsense. He played the way he played. At some point, there was talk that someone hoping to protect the other players would shut him down by injuring him. Nobody had the intestinal fortitude to step up. They were smart enough to give him a wide berth during practice, fearing for their own health if they tried and failed.

Dalmar snapped briefly back to the present and shifted his position in the sea to get more comfortable. He looked up at the sun to determine the time as he tried to remember how he knew of the plot to hurt him all those years ago. Ah, yes. His teammate Nadif Tenge decided he would be much better off aligned with Dalmar than with the rest of the team, so he informed Dalmar of the hatching plots. A wise decision. Next evening Dalmar waited for his new friend, Nadif, to make an early exit from the locker room inside the team's training facilities. Dalmar nodded a brief greeting, then casually barred the paint chipped green doors from the outside and locked them. He picked up three or four homemade bottle rag bombs and lofted them through an open bathroom window. Within eighteen minutes, every player, three coaches, and one trainer were locked permanently in what would become their team coffin. Before the smoke cleared, Dalmar and Nadif Tenge moved on to another life.

****

By the time Dalmar had had as much as he could stand of imitating flotsam, after about twenty-four hours of treading water, a small five-man fishing vessel came into view. He hailed them, and no surprise to him, they heard, responded, and came alongside him. One burly fisherman hoisted Dalmar over the side and the men nodded gravely as he spun a tale of being kidnapped by pirates and left for dead. They gave him blankets and food and a place to sleep for the night while they headed back to shore. About two minutes after Dalmar was certain the men slept, he crushed their skulls, one by one, and pitched their bodies overboard. Revenge still the foremost thought in his mind; he piloted the boat to shore where he called his old loyal friend Nadif.

"I got something I need to get done," he said into the phone.

"When and where?" was all Nadif needed to know.

Within forty-eight hours the two had assembled weapons, a group of men, and two women. Seventy-two hours later they were at sea, making a dead run toward the *Sea Wolf*. Before the next day ended, they boarded her. They slaughtered the crew, letting only the captain and his three top assistants live — for the moment.

At sunrise he put a couple of bullets into the captain's knees and hung the man by his ankles, dangling him overboard like Dalmar had been only one week earlier. *Sweet.*

"I'm not as foolish as you, my captain. You won't escape. Be assured that after you're dead, I'll chop you into shark chum so at least your life won't be totally useless."

One of the other three men peed himself, weeping like a school girl.

"A pirate ship is no place for the weak," Dalmar told him. He shot the man in both shoulders, tossed him overboard, and turned to the last two men.

"As for you two, I would like one of you to go back to town and let everyone know what you just witnessed. Tell them Captain Dalmar is in charge of the *Sea Wolf* and only those with the toughest skins will be allowed to work on her. Those who do can share in what will be her considerable bounty."

He motioned for his crew to drop a life raft. After the last two men were lowered, he tossed them a full canteen and a single can of beans. He removed all but one bullet from a pistol and dropped the weapon between the men.

"There's enough food and water for one man. You decide which of you it's to be."

As the *Sea Wolf* shoved off and left the men adrift, Dalmar turned away and stared into the sun. He smiled when he heard a lone gun shot and then a splash. *Amusing,* he thought, *and actually a bit surprising they were so quick about it.*

CHAPTER TWO

Cullen Nickles had never been greedy about his desire to kill. In fact he'd been downright logical and supremely creative about what he thought of as his *compulsion*. His first and foremost theory in the art of serial killing was that he should not get caught. He would never spend a night in jail, or worse give his dear wife, Elaine, a moment's stress over him even being *accused* of any crime. The way to do that, he always thought, was not to behave like other serial killers. He had no need for mementos or trinkets from his kills. He switched methods as often as possible. He never established a pattern, and he most certainly did not use the same geographical location each time. He liked to refer to himself, again internally, as *the world's foremost international serial killer*. To accomplish this mission a lot of things had to go his way — and things go your way when you plan for them to do so.

Cullen was a large, broad-shouldered man with a warm, knowing smile and a demeanor that allowed him to get close to the most trusting people. He could join into or start any conversation and quickly be the dominating personality. He'd offer a firm handshake, a quick smile that sometimes made it all the way to his eyes, or a compliment to the loneliest person in a room.

Cullen swiped his fingers through his thin brownish-red and white hair. In his heyday, that hair had been full, thick, and extremely attractive to women. The receding fringe didn't bother him because he knew they still found him irresistible. A word or two in his assured voice, deep and slow, with a finish like the words were formed low-down and had to make their way through gravel to get out of his mouth, was all it took to land them. Sexy. He exuded confidence in any situation, making him strongly attractive, he knew that. Result? An easy access to prospective victims.

Cullen had not come to his serial talents in the same way most others do. He knew the prevailing theory that most serial killers come from abusive or neglectful homes, even homes where sexual abuse is the norm. Those losers learn a pattern of repeating abuse; maybe they begin with torturing and murdering small animals. Their pleasure, the thrill of the kill, intensifies and their desire takes them to bigger prey until they, inevitably, seek human prey.

His thoughts drifted, faded, as he felt heat rise in him and beads of sweat pool across his greasy forehead. He swiped at the droplets and wiped his hand on his pants, thinking, *I'm not stupid like them or needy like them.* He thought it pathetic that most serial killers took souvenirs from victims in order to relive the crime at will. That was the perfect way to get caught. The perfect way to leave a trail the most inept cop could follow.

Cullen had a photographic memory. Who needed trinkets or pictures? *His* snapshots and collectables were permanently stored away in the impenetrable vault that was his mind. He could recall them at any time, wherever he was, or whenever he needed them. He defied anyone to trace such mementos.

He smiled as he thought of his own family, practically perfect, a loving family with lots of non-abused pets. The family did nearly everything together. Dinners were pleasant, arguments few and far between. Mr. and Mrs. Nickels seldom, if ever, disciplined Cullen and his twin brother, Cameron, because the boys behaved as expected.

Cullen and Cam were inseparable. They took music lessons side-by-side, played on the same Little League teams, and shared the same group of friends.

By far, the best times were vacations with mom and dad. He remembered shooting photographs of the Grand Canyon and Yellowstone National Park. He had felt well-off and privileged when they spent a week in the Hawaiian Islands and the Rocky Mountains showed him what power and might look like. He learned something new about himself on countless weekend trips, each one better than the one before. Since then, traveling, in and of itself, infused Cullen with a natural high.

Cullen's father, George, was a tall wiry man with light brown hair and a perpetual smile he handed down to his sons. A banking executive, he attended to appearances and never smoked, rarely took a drink. George was well known in the community and among co-workers as an even-tempered, fair man. Friends called him, "The Judge," and asked him to officiate any debates that came up in the group. He laughed a lot and always seemed to be having fun.

Cullen's mother, Shirley, worked in the same bank. She was about a foot shorter than Cullen's dad, but beyond that they shared a lot of traits and qualities. Shirley had a sensitivity toward other people's problems and would never have thought to turn away from anyone in need.

Nickels family time was never compromised by one parent working late or on weekends. The bank had strict policies: No overtime, and no taking work home. Banking management considered staff a collective family and wanted the families within their corporate family to flourish. That is exactly what Cullen's parents wanted, and so their work life helped them support the perfect home life. Cullen reflected now on that perfection as he stared out the window of his home office. He remembered how every spring his mom and dad would sign him and Cameron up for baseball and then co-coach the team. *Everything* was equal, always. Dad might have known more about baseball than mom, but she

18

understood young kids better and could motivate them to play and behave properly. They were, together, the perfect coach. During the season in which Cullen and Cameron would turn nine years old, a league official came to a practice session.

"Mr. and Mrs. Nickels," he said, as he approached the two with his hand outstretched to shake with them each in turn. "I need a favor. Would you mind taking on a player from another team? His dad had a bit of a run in with their coach. It's been ongoing, something about not enough playing time, and the dad requesting moving to another team at the end of last season. I haven't a clue what happened, but someone messed up and the kid got back on the same team."

"A shame it got so far," George said. "There's no other solution?"

"Nope," came the reply. "I'm afraid the dad made a lot of noise and the coach felt threatened. We'd like to fix this before it erupts into something nasty. I don't want to judge anyone or take sides, but I know you folks are great with people and I thought you'd be the right place to turn. I just don't want to see anyone get hurt or tempers escalate. The dad has been pretty clear about his anger."

George looked over at Shirley and accepted her slight nod of assent. With a friendly pat to the man's shoulder, George agreed, no doubt feeling he and his wife could handle anyone.

During their first practice session with Devin, the new boy, Mr. and Mrs. Nickels realized the child's anger mirrored the father's. Neither man nor boy managed their feelings well. The boy's self-control was non-existent. The Nickels interceded numerous times when the kid grabbed or punched a teammate. Devin had a problem with every

request made of him. He boasted.

"Yeah, man, I know how to throw a ball. I don't need

anybody telling me."

No one could possibly show him a better way to hit,

run or throw, and he stood adamant against any sort of

direction, unless, of course, he got the nod from his ever-

present, ever-vigilant father. Still, Cullen's parents kept on

task, feeling they would handle this disruption as they had

others.

"Yo, Devin," George said one afternoon, jogging up to

the kid and offering a smile, "Your dad has some great

methods! You're lucky to have his input. I know, too, that in

baseball, as in life, there are all kinds of ways to get the job

done. But, listen, I need you to give our methods a try and

kind of think about them as though they *will* work, ok? After a fair try, you can decide which makes you feel more comfortable, more capable, ok?"

George's strategy lasted for all of two practices.

On the evening of the third practice, the boy's father, clearly drunk and agitated, wondered in a booming voice from the behind the fence, "Hey! You coaches got your heads up your asses or what?"

He echoed through the small crowd of spectators and across the diamond. Other parents stopped conversations and went silent in the middle of calling encouragement to their kids. A few slid down a few feet on the bleachers and turned their attention back to the game as one dad suggested gently that the heckler relax a little. That brought increasingly vulgar comments which soon developed violent overtones. Parents left the bleachers, putting as much distance as possible between themselves and the drunk. The summer air crackled with tension.

Cullen and his team were fascinated, maybe a little intimidated. Cullen remembered watching his dad shrug at his mom, then jog toward the stands to see if he could diffuse the situation. Mom grouped the team at shortstop and began practice drills. No worries. Dad, as everyone knew, was skilled at smoothing troubled waters. And so, George, keeping the first base side fence between him and Devin's father, was obviously saying something reasonable and non-threatening. No one could hear their conversation, but it appeared as though Cullen's dad made some progress.

While the two men talked and gestured, they held the crowd's attention, but Cullen felt like the electricity in the air had stopped vibrating. Other's seemed to feel the same change. Shirley and the team focused on drilling, while spectators returned to casual conversation and the evening's tone seemed to be one of pleasant community togetherness once more.

Completely unnoticed, Devin separated from the team and trotted casually over to his bat bag in the third base dugout. No one saw him remove something and palm it, cradling the object as though it were fragile and important. Devin put one foot in front of the other, time and again, and crossed the field as though he were in a trance. Still, no one glanced his way. Rising up tall and straight on the pitcher's mound, he raised his hand on outstretched arm at shoulder height. Cullen would never forget how the sun glinted off the small gun Devin steadied with both hands.

Cameron saw the weapon in the same second Cullen did. Both boys were rooted, Cameron's mouth wouldn't open, a scream trapped in his throat. Cullen watched, eyes darting from Cameron to the gun and back. He worked his jaw but couldn't find a way to make sound come out of his mouth.

Cameron shrieked a sound like a police siren, "Dad!" To Cullen, the word had way too many syllables and it felt odd that he observed that.

Cullen heard his brother cough out another sound which became a shriek that sounded as though it would never end. People turned their heads in slow motion, each movement seeming to jerk as a single frame of a movie that wouldn't project properly. Then, time snapped into normal speed and Cullen watched Cameron bolt across the diamond towards the boy with the gun. His every muscle tingled as he fought to move and intervene.

"Daaaaaaad!" The scream followed the hysterical twin and Devin's concentration broke for a nanosecond. In a single motion, he pivoted and ripped a .38 caliber projectile into Cameron's skull, severing the optic nerve, pulverizing facial bone and tissue and shredding through the sinus cavity. The bullet stopped, no more than the width of a sand grain from the carotid artery, and Cam dropped, motionless on the Little League diamond.

Cameron Nickels clung to life for several weeks, clearly not wanting to die, clearly as attached to his perfect family as they were to him. On the fifty-fourth day he died without warning, without change, without reason. George and Shirley never recovered from their emotional wounds; their perpetual smiles and do-good attitudes eroded into permanent depression. Cullen learned about his photographic memory. The graphic gore of his brother's demolished face and then the weeks of him lying in a hospital room played over and over on a loop in his brain. With each iteration, the loop seared scars into the core of Cullen's being.

CHAPTER THREE

Gunnar Fredrickson exemplified a rare breed in his profession. He was the captain of a cruise ship, and he was an American. Most ships are staffed with workers from around the globe, but few American's lined up for the jobs. Americans are unlikely to work for miniscule wages common while climbing the ladder to cruise industry success. Americans seem unwilling to spend six months or a year at sea cramped in a little room with three strangers. They want to quit at five p.m. and go home each night, collecting their Friday paychecks every week. So, plain and simple, cruise lines don't often dole out Captaincies to Americans.

On the other hand, cruise ships are packed with American passengers' intent on spending their paychecks and then some. At some point, Oceanic Airlines and Railways (OAR) acquiesced to surveys filled out by largely

American clientele, and looked around for an American captain. They selected Gunnar and found themselves quite pleased with their decision. Gunnar Fredrickson, who liked to be addressed as Captain Gunnar, proved more than capable as the man in charge of one of their vessels.

He believed in firmly consistent management methods balanced by a good dose of fun. Most importantly, Gunnar related to passengers in an exceptional way. He eschewed stereotypes of ship captains and declined sporting the obligatory tightly-cropped captain's beard. He hated formal uniforms and wore them only when completely unavoidable. Uniform or not, Gunnar commanded attention on any deck or bridge. His dark eyes smoldered with a quick intelligence and thorough understanding of most situations. A sculptured chin cleft drew attention to his swarthy attractiveness.

This day, Gunnar leaned firmly against a sharp sea wind on the foredeck. At six foot four, he stood a head or more above any captain in the fleet and his well-exercised frame, muscled and lean, made him feel like the line's rock star. The wind came at him again and tossed his black hair around in annoying wisps. He shoved the hair back and considered shaving it all off so he wouldn't ever have to mess with a comb or fight the wind's assault. Shrugging, thoughts moving full-speed, he turned up the gangway toward the upper deck basketball courts where he was a familiar site to passengers and staff.

Gunnar had a few minutes and decided to conscript a couple passengers for a pick-up game. Maybe this afternoon he'd have his Cruise Director set up a tournament — passengers versus management. He enjoyed those contests and played his top game every time, but he was no fool. Gunnar knew enough to keep the customers satisfied, and he always found a way to ensure a passenger win in the final game. They practically pissed themselves with delight when they went home. Bragging rights about defeating the ship's captain made for marketing success and trumped the captain's need to score. This morning, he played for about half an hour and then excused himself, claiming duties needed attention.

As he turned, a young cocktail waitress, new on this trip, flashed him a brilliant smile and threw him a wink. He smiled shyly, then turned and stepped quickly in the other direction. *She'd learn*, he thought.

No one thought of him as handsome, but his self-confidence and stature enticed women everywhere. A nuisance sometimes. He made it known to his staff that the sea was his mistress and his wife. They mostly took that to mean he was gay, so for the most part the staff kept their distance. He didn't care what they thought as long as he kept his professional demeanor and their respect.

Female passengers flirted and propositioned, too. He figured it was, for each woman, a case of *what happens on board stays on board.* But Gunnar guarded his private life and kept it private. He'd seen top officers, even captains, lose careers because they had sex, or didn't have sex, with some passenger or another. He refused to jeopardize his career.

Gunnar, who put loyalty above most virtues, stood by his people when they needed him. He never hesitated to recommend them for positions on other ships when he believed they were ready for career advancement. He learned these principles at the U.S. Merchant Marine Academy. After graduating, he spent years working his way across various positions on ships here and there, readying himself to assume his own command. Beyond his assorted duties as he honed his craft, he took care to learn ship technology by spending countless hours with engineers. The

soft-skills, hotel and hospitality, he learned under the wings

of Sophia Caltimano, a gorgeous, seductive, brilliant Italian.

She was twice his age, but he managed to fall in love with

her a long time ago.

Sophia had sensed his fondness and had reciprocated,

allowing herself to be drawn in. But after a short flirtation,

she stunned him with clear-headed practicality.

He'd never forget that day. He heard her voice exude

a sultry smoke, her heavy accent as sexy as anything he had

ever heard. "My lover," she had said, "work must be

separate from love. No matter what we feel for a co-worker

or a passenger, dearest, we must always be able to walk

away before it gets hot."

Standing close, she slipped her hand to the back of his

neck and toyed with his hair, curling it around her finger.

"Never allow anyone to drag you by the penis into

something you cannot get out of with your brain. You understand, my Gunny?"

He had refused, at the time, to understand and he drowned in devastation. Later, he came to his senses about what she meant and he decided to follow the philosophy of his lovely Sophia.

Brushing away the nostalgia, Captain Gunnar continued to circumnavigate the decks of his ship, lending a hand with a mop or a window squeegee if an employee needed help. Sometimes he enjoyed serving the delectable gourmet dishes on the buffet lines; it kept him in touch with activities on his ship. But this day he had more to do. Gunnar was confident his staff and crew never felt spied on or patronized, they shared the cruise experience with him and he liked the family feel of it.

This from a captain who had no family other than his first cousin, Christopher, on his mother's side. Christopher was an only child who had, early on, lost his own mother to breast cancer. Both boys were raised by overbearing fathers and shared the challenge of trying to escape the consequences of such relationships. As an adult, Gunnar kept no home or apartment ashore. When he chose to take his time off, five or six weeks per year, he headed for Christopher's house in Atlanta. Once settled in, he would likely wander, catching a cab to the airport and jetting to cities where he could move around on foot or by taxi. He had no driver's license. *Ironic* he thought; *a man who steers ships weighing in excess of one-hundred and fifty thousand tons cannot drive a car.*

Home didn't mean much to Gunnar. *Why would it?* Again, his thoughts drifted back through time. When Gunnar was seven, Ricky, his older brother by four years, had a group of friends over after school one day. Gunnar's and Ricky's dad was at work. Their mom was in the basement doing laundry. Gunnar played with his dad's tools and watched TV in the basement while Mom busied herself with laundry. She folded piles of fresh-smelling clothes and chatted with him as she worked on the homey task.

Ricky and his buddies must have gotten tired of race cars and cap guns. Later, it was clear that the desire for excitement drew Ricky to his parent's closet where he was never allowed to play or explore. But he knew what was in there. What eleven year-old could resist showing off forbidden fruit? Ricky had climbed a shelf to pull down a closed, sturdy shoe box. Inside lay his father's gun and some stray bullets that rolled and clanked around the bottom of the box. The boys passed the gun to each other for a few moments. What could happen? Clearly, the bullets hadn't been loaded into the gun.

The game escalated. They took turns, aiming the small black gun at each other, "Kapow!"

One boy mocked putting it against his own head, yelled "Boooom!" and laughed raucously. Each time someone pretended to fire, a shiver of fun fear tingled inside every small body.

The bullet that killed Ricky exploded into his face. It rammed him back through the rack of clothes and against the rear wall. The force catapulted him forward and his small frame dropped face down at the feet of three little boys frozen with fear. It took agonizing moments for Mrs. Fredrickson to sprint up the stairs. That unmistakable sound reverberated in her head. She wasn't even cognizant of little Gunnar struggling to keep up with her terrified dash.

Three boys were still frozen on their feet. One small body was motionless on the floor. A spreading pool of blood crawled across white carpet. Gunnar remembered wondering why the blood looked dark, almost black, instead of red like on TV.

After this long, Gunnar could still replay in living color his mother on her knees, rolling his brothers body over. A gaping hole replaced Ricky's nose and right eye. Gunnar remembered recognizing his mother's anguish when she first looked up at him through her beautiful hair fallen over her blue, blue eyes. He still could watch three boys turn and run — out of the room, down the stairs, through the front door — all in slow motion. But he couldn't have seen all that, could he? He had stayed in the closet as they fled, wishing it was darker than it actually was.

Days, weeks, months passed without a word spoken in his house. His mother turned cold eyes on his father, and Gunnar knew she held him accountable. They had argued so many times about keeping a gun in the house. One year to the day after her son was buried, Mrs. Fredrickson, by then a mushy lump of a nonperson, took the same gun that had killed her son and turned it on herself.

Gunnar survived, and when it was time, he went to sea. Somewhere in his twenty-fifth year of life, he got word that his father had passed. It was weeks after the death before the message found Gunnar and there seemed no reason to go home. Why return to a home that had ceased to be? So he stayed aboard, did his job, and made every effort to wipe from his memory all that had passed.

CHAPTER FOUR

I'm losing my mind, thought Joanne Sampson as she rushed around the house in pre-vacation frenzy. *I can't remember if I packed my curling iron.* She jammed a paperback book and a couple of magazines into her carry-on bag.

"Jen, did you pack your curling iron?" she shouted to her sixteen year-old, who always seemed vaguely amused at her mother's frenetic purposefulness.

"Of course — I couldn't live without that thing," Jen replied, walking into the room. "Don't worry. If yours doesn't turn up, you can use mine. No big deal."

That was just like Jennifer, she was always the calm in the storm. She had very few of the parent issues most teenagers bitched about. Jen wasn't embarrassed to be around her parents — they were awesome, made her feel proud a lot of the time.

Her dad was a veterinarian with a thriving practice.

This worked in Jen's favor. Throughout her school years, he

frequently volunteered to talk about his career and often

brought animals into her classrooms. The other kids loved

Doctor Steve, a localized version of Jack Hannah sharing

knowledge of unique critters in a natural way with no

talking down to kids, ever. If a bird fell out of a tree in Jen's

neighborhood, it was always, "Call Doctor Steve." If

someone found a squirrel with a broken leg, Dr. Steve would

be alerted before anyone else. Jennifer loved that their

community trusted her dad and respected him. Without her

being much aware of it, that trust and respect that her father

had earned had trickled onto her reputation, as well. She

was so highly regarded and mature for her age, that by

eleven she was working in her father's office helping out

nurturing and caring for abandoned animals the veterinary

center seemed to attract. By thirteen she had set up a

program in which she weaned and then later found homes for injured and helpless kittens. The harder cases she stuck with as long as possible, until she could find no further solutions.

Jen still wasn't clear why her mom and dad had divorced about a year earlier, but they had instilled such a sense of security and self-esteem in her that she never took it on herself to feel at fault. The divorce didn't destroy her sense of who she was, or her sense of family. She made the best of whatever she was handed, unlike her worrisome little brother, Robert.

Robby was eight years-old, and he took Dad moving out as a personal affront. Not understanding why he couldn't live in the same house with both parents, Robby was the one who blamed himself. Jen, as usual, played the voice of reason, explaining life to Rob and comforting him when he cried at night. It wasn't that Mom and Dad couldn't or wouldn't provide comfort. Jen did it better.

In Jen, people saw a mini-version of her mother. Physically they were correct, but Jen's personality more closely matched her father's. She inherited his calm demeanor and self-confidence. Her flowing black hair and deeply tan complexion came from her mom. Not among the elite beauties of her school years, she could have been the poster child for cute-and-brainy, with a personality that made her approachable and real. She had more dates than girls stunning in looks and never lacked for friends who valued her opinion and her company. Her mother's never-quit attitude, supported by a backbone of steel, passed to Jen making them both the sort of women who never met a challenge they wouldn't confront head-on and with gusto.

Joanne Sampson developed that attitude during her years working in television newsrooms. She learned most newsrooms were dominated by male personalities. Early on, she decided she would only be heard by displaying more assertiveness, even aggression if necessary, and outshouting those with the biggest mouths.

Joanne started working for the CBS affiliate in Tampa after graduating from the University of Central Florida in Orlando. Hired as an intern in graphics, her enlightened aptitude for news took her rapidly to the newsroom where she spent a few years as a writer, learning the business. Shortly, Joanne made assistant producer, did some time on the assignment desk, and finally landed a spot as the morning show producer. The job meant long hours and lots of time working without supervision, because most of higher management would never consider such early morning hours. This unsupervised time was her opportunity to shine, and she went after the opportunity with cyclone speed and force.

If she couldn't get a photographer because the station was stingy with overtime that month, she'd take it upon herself to find a freelancer. When management called her out on it and refused to pay, she'd foot the bill. She got a lot poorer, but gained legendary status among other employees as a relentless pursuer of whatever story she was after. When a huge story broke about two seven year-olds lost in some woods, Joanne talked her way onto the police search helicopter, and then she trumped all by spotting the boys huddled in the brush. She maneuvered herself into prime position on camera as rescuers guided the kids to safety.

On an impulse, Joanne decided to ride with a photographer to a routine building fire. Not interested in the limelight this time, she hung back with all the gawkers and let the photographer do his job capturing images of flames, and then carnage afterwards. Standing there, she noticed one of the gawkers letting a smile play across his lips. *Odd,* she thought, *it's almost like he's enjoying the fire.* His expression contrasted sharply with other faces turned up in horror. Sprinting to the camera guy, Joanne tugged his sleeve.

"Hey, listen, grab me some crowd reaction, can you?"

He turned and cocked his head from behind the lens.

"W T F, woman?" he growled, losing concentration. He almost turned away, but Joanne saw him rethink it. She knew her reputation with him was solid. When she asked for something, she had a good reason. He complied, panning faces and picking one or two to focus on.

Back at the newsroom, she copied his tape and ran it down to her friends in the police department. The cops recognized her suspicious character as a known arsonist who delighted in watching his fires consume buildings. Within hours the police had him. The next day's headline read: TV Producer's Quick Thinking Nails Arsonist for

Police.

That presence of mind solidified her legendary status,

and launched Joanne smack into a network job. NBC wanted

her as a researcher for their investigative unit. ABC offered

to make her producer for their flash squad, a unit dispatched

anywhere in the world for breaking news. CBS offered her a

spot as assistant producer for the *Nightly News*. Great offers,

all, but she craved the immediacy, the impact of the *Nightly*

News. That suited her.

Off to New York Joanne went and she worked three

years there, ending up as a line producer. A miserable three

years, she recalled, living in the city sucked. At work, she

thrived on the excitement but hated dealing with unions

instead of focusing on her job. You had to be in the writers'

union to report or write news and the electrical union if you

shot pictures or film or served as editor or worked in a

technical capacity. Back home in Tampa nobody cared about unions, they cared about getting the job done. She longed to return and regroup, but loathed taking a step back. About that time, her father had a mild heart attack, giving her the excuse she needed.

"My dad's ill and I need to come back to help take care of him," she told the personnel director at her old station in Tampa.

"Well, welcome back," came the answer, fueling her self-esteem and erasing all thoughts of failure. She hung up the phone and immediately began planning her exit strategy.

Within a month, she was producing the CBS affiliate's public affairs program called, *The Pulse of Tampa Bay*. She knew she had chosen wisely those eighteen years ago. Within eighteen months of resettling in Tampa, she'd met Steve and married him. They'd had Jennifer that same year. As time passed, Joanne entrenched herself in community relations writing and reporting, letting heavy-handed news fall to others. Her bulldog nature evolved into something milder — still assertive, still competent and rock-steady — but tamer. Joanne had no doubt she could resurrect that fierce bulldog if she ever desired to jump back into the newsroom, and her colleagues would have agreed.

CHAPTER FIVE

During the past seven years, mostly due to the popularity of his television commercials, James Billington III had been named America's most famous and trusted corporate leader at least six times by *Executive Magazine*. He was recognized as one of America's richest men, with a net worth of slightly more than a billion dollars. Not bad for a guy who really had never done much of anything. According to the *real* top executives running the company, he still wasn't doing much of anything except collecting large checks, getting in the way, and taking total credit for the company's recent run of extreme success.

He had come into his money and his company the old fashioned way. He inherited everything. His grandfather, James Billington, had started the company in the 1940's with one ship that delivered goods from New York to London. As the first Billington's customer base grew, they wanted more and quicker deliveries, so he acquired more ships and branched out to shipping products from ports in Baltimore and Miami. When he discovered the benefits and profits of shipping across the United States, he purchased a rail company and expanded business on the ground. When he knew air shipping was the next big thing he purchased a small fleet of planes and the company became air-born, too. By the 1960's, James Billington Jr. stepped in to run Billington Freight, one of the largest shipping organizations in the world.

The second Billington proved to be an even greater visionary than his father. He envisioned a scenario in which his ships carried passengers to destinations all around the world, and his airline brought people to his ships. He even figured a way to fix up train cars and get people to pay for passage around the country. In the late sixties, this Billington took the family name off the company, changing it to *OAR* for Oceans-Airlines-Railways. They offered cheaper, all-inclusive vacations that often took people from OAR trains to OAR planes and then to OAR ships. Though the firm still continued in the shipping business, it wasn't long before vacation cruising sales dwarfed all other aspects of the company's profile and bottom line.

In the early 1970s, when James Billington Jr. died suddenly and unexpectedly in a boating accident, his son, James Billington III, was only twenty-one. He was not yet ready to take over the company, so it was entrusted to a Billington cousin who promptly sold off the shipping divisions along with the airplanes and rail interests. This decision gutted OAR for the long term and made the cousin incredibly wealthy. By the time James Billington III was ready to take over there was only a single aspect of the business to concentrate on. Unfortunately, he wasn't all that good at even one focus.

During Billington III's twenty-some years' run as president, OAR spiraled downward at an ever-quickening pace. He faced options of selling the company outright or bringing in management to jump start business into new directions. More interested in money than in establishing any reputation as a great business man, he dug up investors who understood and embraced the burgeoning cruise travel business. The new blood funneled a fair amount of new capital into building ships and into refurbishing older ships. OAR soon enjoyed reaping profits of a fruitful renaissance.

Meanwhile, James Billington III became nothing more than a figurehead who appeared in television commercials and print advertisements. James had zero business acumen, but he could sell an idea better than anyone. He sported an intentional down-to-earth believable style, and, despite his great wealth, came on like any working man who needed a vacation.

The commercial spots usually depicted him lounging on one of his cruise ships or sipping an exotic drink in a tropical location. Sometimes, he cracked open a lobster shell with endearing ineptness in a resort dining room or clumsily rode on a horse to showcase one of the many excursions offered to guests on OAR cruises. Not long after the first commercials aired, *Time Magazine* ran a cover story with his picture and the question, *Is This America's Most Trusted Executive?* That week, his popularity soared to great heights and the commercials took on an even more humorous bent. He'd be shown getting into a bit of trouble only to be saved by a passenger who would inevitably recognize him. The passenger echoed *Time's* query, "Hey, wasn't that America's most trusted executive?"

OAR based operations in Tampa, while Billington enjoyed his main home in South Florida and gravitated among satellite homes in Tampa, Nantucket, and Telluride.

He and his mostly reclusive wife lived with their twin daughters — both Christened with nautical names — Marina and Lorelei. The girls, in their early twenties, showed little desire to get into the family business, and indeed, not much interest in anything beyond South Beach partying and clubbing.

Noting his daughters' apparent indifference to the Billington cash cow, and knowing business would continue to grow and produce said cash, Billington often wondered how his family firm would end up when he had had enough. He could sell it outright and relax for the rest of his days, but his ego fed on his finely honed notoriety. He loved being recognized by people, and it turned him on to kid with his socialite buddies like Donald Trump that Billington's fame outpaced The Donald's. After much ruminating, he decided to someday sell the company and swing a deal in which he stayed on as spokesman. *Nothing could work out better,* he thought. He'd suck up the exposure

he so dearly loved, dump the daily headaches of running

OAR, and make a lot of money. There was one final

puzzlement. He had people in top management who would

jump at taking over the company, but he was never sure

whether he trusted them enough to let that happen.

CHAPTER SIX

At about ten-thirty that morning, Joanne, Jen, and Robby settled into their limo and the driver headed for Tampa's cruise terminal. The trio felt rushed, as all vacationers do, but figured they'd relax at the dock before boarding *the Treasure of the Seas*. They made it to the terminal in plenty of time, but in their rush to make it out the door at home, they'd forgotten the carry-on bag that contained Joanne's laptop, her Kindle, and a few magazines she'd intended to read on the trip. Joanne was annoyed but there wasn't much to be done about the bag.

In the thirteen months since her divorce, Joanne had forgotten quite a few things. As time passed, she realized it wasn't forgetfulness so much as overlooking stuff her now ex-husband would have formerly taken care of. Oddly, she missed that sense of partnership most, though she valued and desired independence above almost everything else. She thought maybe someday she'd marry again, but for now that was a faraway consideration. She devoted her energy and derived her satisfaction from getting her daughter into a good college and spending time with her little Robby. Her decision to end her marriage was dead on right.

This trip on *the Treasure of the Seas* provided a perfect opportunity for the three of them to bond. The cruise would stop in St. Thomas and St. Maarten, then at a private island owned by OAR and situated between the other two islands. Joanne eagerly anticipated catching up on her reading, while Jen couldn't wait to get into her Bikini and tan on tropical beaches. Robby mostly looked forward to twenty-four hour pizza buffets he'd seen highlighted in the brochures.

Jen palmed the phone that seemed a permanent extension of her body and she whipped out several last minute texts to friends letting them know she would be in touch when she arrived at her exotic locations. Without breaking her nimble-fingered stride and without looking up she casually spoke to her mother, "Mom you remembered to switch us over to the international calling plan right? It'll cost us a whole lot less when we get to those tropical islands."

"Of course, dear," her mom replied with a measure of sarcasm. "I've been forgetting a lot of things lately, but I wouldn't think about inhibiting your ability to communicate with the outside world." Half an hour later in the terminal, Robby bubbled with uncontained excitement. Bouncing and fidgeting, he announced he would be in the pool, eating his first slice of pizza, by noon. Joanne wondered whether they could even board yet, but Jen, as usual, had the details all mapped out.

"According to postings on the internet," she said, "You can start boarding as early as eleven, but you won't be able to get into your cabin until about one in the afternoon.

So we can get on board, do some exploring, and maybe get ourselves lunch."

"Sounds like a plan," Joanne said.

"When can we go swimming and get pizza?" Robby pestered for the twentieth time.

But Joanne smiled, not annoyed. She was thrilled her kids were so excited and relieved that they hadn't mentioned or apparently thought about their father at all.

"Don't worry about it, buddy," she said to Robby. "You've got a whole week to eat all the pizza you can cram down."

The moment they mounted the gangway and stepped aboard the ship they felt they were entering a different world. The three of them stood with their mouths agape for a moment, taking in the ship's pristine beauty, before they decided it was alright to move. They had embarked on the eighth of fifteen floors, in the middle of an atrium that stretched below to the fifth floor and above to the ninth.

Glass elevators, sparkling with a hospital-like clean,

transported excited passengers up and down among the

decks. On the floor directly below Joanne and her kids lay

the breathtaking two-story shopping mall. It had several

jewelry stores and clothing stores and a general store where

guests could purchase books and other small items.

Interspersed throughout the deck were various food stands.

To starboard they'd find Dubliners Irish Pub and the Salty

Dog coffee shop. To port side there was an ice cream shop

and the pizza parlor Robby so desperately wanted to try.

The Café, a sandwich shop with a 1927 Model T Ford parked

out front, served free gourmet sandwiches all day long.

Further down the strip, an open piano bar beckoned

visitors to its main attractions, Sir Jon Elton and Mr. Joely

Bill on alternating nights. In reality, both roles were played

by one long-time performer who had been a complete and

utter failure on land yet drew standing ovations and warm responses from crowds at sea.

"Mom," Jen shrieked, "Oh my God! The mall! The brochure didn't do it justice at all! Unbelievable." She grabbed her phone and shot off a few rapid-fire texts to teens less fortunate than herself languishing at home.

"The pizza parlor is down there with the mall! Let's go. Right now!" Robby, off-the-chains excited, simultaneously tugged at his mother and shoved his sister toward the elevators.

None of them noticed a handsome man in uniform standing right in front of them. Most captains take some time off when passengers board or disembark, but not Captain Gunnar. He joined his hospitality staff, smiling and glad-handing distracted travelers. Robby bumped straight into him.

"Well, hello there, young man. What's the rush? You're on vacation," the captain said, smiling. "Chill. I promise you'll get to do everything you want."

"I'm terribly sorry, "Joanne said, catching Captain Gunnar's eye. "We're so excited we forgot our manners."

"Understandable, ma'am. We're here to make your stay the best ever. Don't hesitate to ask for anything you wish. I'm Captain Gunnar Fredrickson. My staff and I are at your service."

He actually did a slight head-bow. Looking up at his considerable stature, Joanne was, for the first time since college days, flustered. She felt a warm flush in her chest. She swallowed and disciplined herself back to normal. He cut an amazing figure in his uniform, and although she'd never subscribed to that man-in-uniform type, she could suddenly see what all the fuss was about.

"Why, thank you, sir. You can call me Jo, and this is my son, Jennifer, and my daughter, Robby." Jen grimaced and rolled her eyes at her mother's mistake, but Captain Gunnar smiled and shook hands with each of them. "How would you guys like to see the ship's bridge at some point during your cruise?" he asked.

"Are you serious?" This from Robby.

"Sure am. Take this card and call the number on it. We'll set it up for you."

"Awesome!" Robby chirped. "I can't believe I already met the captain."

Joanne blushed. "Thank you so much, Captain, we'll certainly take you up on your generous offer." The family turned, and Joanne nodded toward the elevator, steering her little brood and trying to avoid any more collisions as their eyes danced from this view to that amenity.

"Really, mom? *Jo*? You told him to call you *Jo*! I've never heard you ask anyone to call you *Jo*. It sounds like you already got yourself a man friend," Jen taunted.

Joanne, still blushing and warm, brushed her hair off her face with one hand and steered her daughter with the other. "Well maybe it's time to make a few lifestyle changes. Don't you think?" A secret smile played at her lips.

As the trio moved through the atrium, Captain Gunnar knew he was about to break every rule he'd ever written for himself. What he was thinking was wrong on so many levels. As he'd chatted with Jo, he'd briefly wondered if a husband and father would be joining this family, but he saw no rings on Jo's fingers. All this went through Captain Gunnar's careful, cautious mind at lightning speed and, feeling his legs weaken, he made an aggressive move entirely out of character. His mouth called out before his mind was ready to speak.

"Ah Jo, would you and your family like to dine with me at the Captain's table this evening?

The tiniest hesitation played at Joanne, and then, without a thought about consulting her family, "We'd be honored Captain." She realized her mistake, and turned to the kids. "Wouldn't we, guys? I mean dinner at the Captain's table on our first night? Sounds great, doesn't it?"

"Yeah, awesome! Can I have pizza?"

"You can have anything you'd like, young man, as long as it's alright with your mom," the Captain said. "What's your cabin number, so I can have someone escort you to my table this evening?"

"We're in ninety-five zero-zero," Jen said. They exchanged a smile and Gunnar nodded. He turned his head while extending his hand in greeting to the next vacationer coming his way. Joanne and company boarded a glass elevator and kept up lively conversation as they saw more of the ship from their vantage points. They were blown away by the view of a part of the multi- level dining room spanning decks four, five and six. Giant marble pillars with sculptured cupids attached rose through all three decks, looking like they were floating above the diners and observing them while they ate. Hundreds of tables accommodated groups of two or twelve or anything in between. Early diners were seated promptly at six, and late dining was at eight. Dinner entertainment might be a professional presentation or the servers and assistants dancing and singing. The company overlooked no chance to put a smile on the customers' faces and they required staff to mirror those smiles, always.

CHAPTER SEVEN

For a long time, the *Treasure of the Seas* was the pride of the OAR lines fleet. Though it had recently been surpassed by larger ships with more amenities, it was still a shining jewel of an ocean liner. Weighing in at close to one-hundred and fifty-five thousand tons, it accommodated about thirty-five hundred passengers. The ship was a cruiser's dream; it boasted three pools, eight Jacuzzis, an exercise room with its own boxing ring, a rock climbing wall, and several specialty restaurants among countless other attractions.

The ship's lower exterior was light blue, while the top half always gleamed with freshly painted white. Large open balconies ringed the vessel. *Treasure of the Seas*, lettered in fancy bold script, graced both starboard and port sides toward the bow and the company logo, a globe with the giant letters OAR encircling the earth, was emblazoned on both sides, aft. Two enormous red and black stacks billowed smoke aloft next to a white circular object that looked like a massive golf ball. The golf ball housed sensitive satellite communications equipment. While the outside of the ship was impressive, the grandeur of the interior layers trumped that impression.

Treasure's capacity of several thousand passengers approximated the population of a tiny town or city and some cruises spanned as long as two weeks, more if there were delays. Such an imposing habitat, at a thoroughly imposing price point, required all the perks, luxuries, and amenities necessary for any dream vacation. This palace on water had hundreds of luxury cabins, ranging from single accommodations to celebrity suites, strategically located throughout fourteen immense decks.

At least a half dozen restaurants ensured that diners always left their tables with smiles on their faces. Cuisine was top notch and amongst the best at sea with selections

guaranteed to present passengers with challenging culinary

dilemmas every day. Guests could opt for five-star stand-out

restaurants like *The Land*, fine dining on top-class chops and

steaks, or *The Sea*, gourmet fare from the ocean. A quick ride

in glass elevators put diners steps away from entrees like

roast duck, prime rib, mahi-mahi, Maine lobster, fresh pasta,

vegetarian fare, or low-fat delicacies. Ubiquitous to-die-for

desserts were almost obligatory, dieting be damned. That

didn't even consider the abundant and always available

buffets, which warranted a deck to themselves.

Topside, the ship's smallest and highest decks

contained service-oriented amenities like a chapel and an

observation point. The lowest two decks held economically-

sized but comfortable enough crew quarters and the

infirmary. The infirmary, a three room suite where both

crew and guests received medical care, was the only area on

the lower decks where guests were allowed. A reception

room housed medical files, books, and a locked cabinet

containing basic drug items. Reception led to two examining

rooms. The staff treated most patients in the Reef Room,

equipped to deal with excesses of all sorts — food, drink,

sun, or activity — and with sea sickness or food poisoning,

both more prevalent than the cruise industry cared to admit.

The Halyard Room, somewhat larger and with better

lighting, handled overflow or was used for minor surgeries

like stitching a lacerated finger or cleaning up an infected

foot. Staff included three nurses with varying degrees of

experience and expertise and one incompetent physician

with a desire to escape from life's challenges.

On deck five, at the back of the ship, was the lower

level of the Billington Palace where nightly Vegas-style

shows featured singers, dancers, magicians, and rotating

variety acts. Towards the middle of deck five, Lucky Seven

Casino gave gaming enthusiasts the latest video poker and electronic slot machines, blackjack tables, craps tables, roulette wheels, stud poker, and hundreds of other games of chance. A large bar area with enormous flat screen televisions offered betting opportunities on almost any sporting event the world over. Other decks located above and below housed activities and entertainment for all ages and any level of physical fitness, from kids to retirees. Adult passengers weren't allowed on one particular supervised decked where kids and teens had the freedom to work off a bit of steam and forge vacation friendship bonds. A few specialty guest cabins and suites were tucked in strategic locations on various decks, but the majority of regular cabins lined decks four through six, with suites on nine. The Joanne, Jen and Rob Sampson's family cabin, 9500, was on deck nine directly aft, which meant in the far back corner of the ship. The room had a view of the wake from the balcony as the vessel glided through the ocean. In many ways, the Sampson's location made it easier for them to get their bearings on such an expansive ship. Their accommodation, one of six on the small corridor, was considered a Junior Suite.

When the three arrived at their accommodations, Jen approved the three-hundred square feet and an additional hundred square feet of private balcony. She laid claim to the queen size bed; Joanne and Robbie would share the couch that converted into an extra bed. A flat-screen television occupied the wall space above a small desk. The clean and modern bathroom contained a shower so small it looked like the cabin would flood if the ship tilted while someone ran the water. Robby thought it a perfect size for him but wondered how any normal-sized adult could fit in it to take a poop.

The family quickly put away their clothes in creatively placed ample storage spaces and stowed their luggage under the bed. The cabin wasn't overly large, but they were determined to spend as little time in it as possible, so it would do.

Exploring the corridor, Robby noticed 9502, to the left of the Sampson's room, was the same size with an identical balcony. Since the door was latched open, he decided it was unoccupied. He walked on past open doors of 9504 and 9506, Royal Suites, substantially larger than his family's Junior Suite. Growing bored with his self-directed tour, Robby yelled over his shoulder, "Hey you guys, let's *do* something!"

Jen, Joanne, and Robby headed off to begin their voyage and their adventures. Cullen Nickels, burning with desire to accomplish his mission, settled himself and his wife

Elaine into Royal Suite 9504 — two doors down from the

Sampson's room.

CHAPTER EIGHT

Eighteen months earlier. Gulf of Aden — between Somalia and Yemen.

Abdi Dalmar, along with his first mate Nadif Tenge and their crew, had just completed a one-month negotiation that had netted them more than five million American dollars. They'd seized an oil tanker and held its crew hostage, not an easy operation. In recent years, a fleet of international warships cruised a daily patrol in the Gulf of Aden. If they thought certain ships were being shadowed by pirate vessels, the warships could provide escort for many miles. Abdi Dalmar and his pirates had to continuously come up with faster, more efficient ways to capture their prey. Usually, they launched two or three small, speedy boats from their master pirate vessel. They'd overtake slower ships and board them quickly in a hail of gunfire and smoke.

Because captive crews' lives could be worth as much as ships' cargo, dummy bullets served as enough distraction to allow pirates to board, secure the crew for later ransom while avoiding a collection of worthless dead bodies. Men on those ships were so valuable that small villages had cropped up along the Somalia coast to accommodate hostages. Newly erected restaurants fed them and, in this opportunistic and entrepreneurial economy, the hostages enjoyed decent housing accommodations. Rarely were captives mistreated. Pirates of Somalia did quite well for themselves. They drove expensive cars, built luxurious houses, and filled their leisure time with beautiful women. They bankrolled businesses; both legitimate and not, hired accountants, and purchased ever-growing collections of state-of-the-art weaponry from typical fringe elements.

Most pirates would say they got into it for the best of reasons, refusing to see themselves as bad guys. How could they be labeled undesirable? They didn't pollute their oceans with illegal waste dumps or overfish their seas, as so many others did. Somalia's once tuna-rich waters had been overfished by commercial fisherman from a multitude of countries. So, a few years ago, enterprising Somalia fisherman considered themselves forced to take up arms and become ocean vigilantes, confronting whatever greedy boat captains they could accost and demanding tax payments. That was then. Now, a growing, streamlined operation forged with good intentions was overflowing with very, very bad intentions.

The Somalia government, always transitional and virtually non-existent for years had zero capability of stopping or even interfering with pirates of any sort. The few government officials who managed to hang on to shreds of power knew better than to mess with pirates. Those tin soldiers found themselves only too happy to accept bribe money.

Abdi Dalmar grew filthy rich as a pirate. He kept his collections of fine wines and gorgeous cars at a lavish hillside estate overlooking the ocean. Dalmar had other collections — art, rare fish, and exotic women. Oddly, once he possessed anything he completely lost interest in it. His sole aspiration was to possess more of everything than anyone else could. Dalmar's drive, his moment-by-moment motivation, sprung from his hatred of anything human. He barely tolerated people, even his most loyal and trusted mate, Nadif. Dalmar lusted after dominating and destroying every one he met. He needed to dominate and destroy those who stood up to him as competition. He needed to destroy and dominate anyone the least bit subservient or submissive to him. He tolerated no cowards or fools. Dalmar had felt that way in his early days on the soccer field, and that same angry drive dogged him still whether he captained his ship at sea, or he surveyed his treasures and domain on the land.

As usual, sleep eluded him this night. He dozed for two to three hours and woke. Dalmar didn't mind. He preferred to stay up and surf the Internet, searching for new ways to dominate the sea. The more time he put to effective use while his opponents wasted time sleeping, the closer he moved toward more victories. Obsessively, he studied oceans and companies sending tankers through his region. Utilizing his uncanny intuition and planning instincts, he unerringly situated himself in the right place at the right time. He relished being able to afford hefty bribes for captains of police vessels patrolling his seas, too.

Other pirates, much like his soccer mates of long ago, feared Dalmar because his reputation as a truly bloodthirsty pirate reached everywhere. While most pirate captains learned that hostages were the most important part of a transaction, Dalmar could never resist a kill — at least one hostage had to perish, purely for sport. Usually, he chose to torture the second in command. It felt righteous to slice them open with the Samurai sword he'd acquired during his travels, another possession that bolstered his need to have more. He felt sexually aroused as he observed how long it took for pain to trigger the victim's primordial need to scream. He loved hearing them scream.

Sucking in a deep breath of satisfaction, he would shout at them, "Ha, Baqin! Ha, Ooyin! Do not be afraid! Do not cry!"

When finished with his prey, their gaping wounds pouring blood onto the decks, he'd hoist their bodies up the mast to display them like trophies. The bodies would hang for the duration of negotiations, serving to speed things up nicely. It wasn't unheard of for the second in command of any vessel under pirate attack to jump ship; preferring death in the sea to the risk of what he knew would likely come at the hands of Dalmar. Many a third in command pissed himself after the second leapt to his death. Other pirate captains grew weary of Dalmar's cut throat ways and wanted him out of the way so pirating could settle back down to its former simple processes. But like the soccer players who'd dealt with Dalmar in the past, today's pirates worried about the consequences of failing to end his madness, and so far, no one had risked his wrath.

****

Nadif Tenge slammed down the empty tankard, his twelfth beer in an hour, and relished his dull numbing drunkenness. Tenge sobered up miraculously when someone dragged a dark, heavy canvas bag over his head, obliterating light and almost cutting off his air supply. He fought, clawing at the thick cloth, but two punches to his abdomen and one to his face sucked the wind from his lungs. He feared they had broken his nose. He kicked feebly when his hands and feet were bound; then he was dumped into the trunk of a car. The lid slammed. The motor roared and the vehicle turned and curved so many times he gave up any hope of getting his bearings. When the car stopped and he was hauled out of the trunk, he smelled fire and heard crackling flames while he felt his captors drag him right to the heat source that seared the bag onto his face. They tied a rope to his abdomen and someone, some distance off, pulled it taught. Tenge surmised he was about to be a thrust into the middle of a ring of fire, a persuasive technique he had seen applied to others. A man spoke.

"You are Nadif Tenge?"

Tenge remained silent.

"Tell me," the voice insisted more loudly, "are you not Nadif Tenge, second in command to the pirate, Abdi Dalmar?"

Still, Tenge refused to speak. One second later he felt fire all around him. He was inside the circle now, the rope around his abdomen held by someone outside the ring of fire. Apparently, they had decided they didn't need him to verify his identity.

"We have no interest in games. You will go back to Captain Dalmar and inform him it is time for him to leave the Gulf of Aden. I speak for all captains — we stand together — suggesting strongly he look for employment elsewhere. If he intends to stay and fight, he must fight us all and his crew must be made aware of this. We will kill all of his crew first. Even he cannot stand up to this kind of coalition. If he had played by the rules, there was plenty for all of us, but he has brought too much heat on the entire Gulf."

Tenge decided to speak, "He raised the stakes and the monies for all of you. You should be grateful."

"No! He put us at greater risk with his barbaric ways. You' will survive tonight, so you may convince him there is no turning back from this point. For the sake of all, you *must* be as persuasive with him as we are being with you."

CHAPTER NINE

Cullen and Elaine Nickels encountered the Sampson family for the first time as they all stood just outside their cabins, about to unlock and lock their respective doors. Cullen, dressed in cruise casual Khaki pants and a Hawaiian shirt, had painstakingly arranged his hair in a comb-over to conceal thinness and a large, expanding bald area. Hoping to appear youthful, he wore simple loafers with no socks. Actually, Cullen looked to be in his early fifties though he had just celebrated his sixty-fourth birthday. The man's easy-going, laid back air complemented his infectious smile.

Elaine tended to a more conservative look in a red, Sarah Palin style jacket paired with a nautical scarf that coordinated with a nautical handbag. Joanne thought Elaine's white gloves oddly formal and out-of-date, but she would later learn that the woman's gambling obsession necessitated the gloves for sanitation. Most casinos had made it unnecessary to yank one-armed bandit slot machine levers years ago, but Elaine continued to do it because she loved the sensation of the gloves on her hands and the lever on her gloves.

"Happy cruise!" Robby yelled at the older couple.

"Why thank you, young man," replied Cullen. "Is this your first time aboard the *Treasure of the Seas?*"

"It's our first time aboard anything that floats," Jen cut in.

"I'm gonna have dinner with the captain tonight, and my mom is now called Jo," Robby informed them in a rush.

"I'm sorry" Joanne said, tugging at a large piece of luggage positioned by their door. "Is my little guy bothering you?"

"Not at all," Cullen said to her, and turned back to Robby and Jen. "I've been on more than thirty of these cruises. Anytime you'd like me to regale you with cruising stories, let me know."

His mind dwelled on people he'd murdered on these trips and he smiled, knowing he wouldn't share those stories.

"He'll bore you to death," Elaine cut in. "Run the other way if he tries to tell you his foolish stories — or his jokes, for that matter."

"Oh, come on," Cullen said. "My stories are killers."

Again, his inner thoughts tickled him. As Elaine walked into the room with her carry bag, Cullen whispered to the Sampson's, "Don't listen to her, she's a big drinker." He put his right thumb to his lips and sucked a swig from an imaginary bottle.

"I heard that, you pain in the neck," Elaine hollered from inside.

"She's got ears like a bear," Cullen whispered.

"I heard that, too."

Cullen smiled, lifted both hands as though surrendering, shrugged his shoulders and followed his wife into their cabin.

After shutting the door and puttering around for a moment or two, he walked out on to the verandah, thinking about how much he loved cruising. He thought about how much he loved his wife, and he thought about how much he loved to plunge a knife into a human's heart. Years ago, he'd established his rules of killing and had figured out why a cruise vacation offered him the greatest cover. It helped that Elaine was an addicted gambler and never got off the ship — no need to dream up excuses or explanations. Once they got on a boat, they saw each other at dinner and briefly connected in the cabin before retiring for the evening. He liked knowing she had thoughts for nothing other than her gaming. He giggled to himself, watching the sea, feeling its rhythm, and thinking of what a symbiotic pair he and his spouse were.

Elaine liked to sleep in. Cullen rose at the crack of morning light. Elaine stayed out late. Cullen retired early. Elaine liked to gamble. Cullen wouldn't be caught dead in a casino. Elaine ordered breakfast delivered to their room. Cullen preferred the buffet; he never considered room service. Elaine paired wine with dinner. Cullen rarely drank. Well, when he completed a kill and was satisfied, he treated himself to one of those drinks with a paper umbrella stuck in it. The two of them agreed on a couple things — they loved each other and they both adored vacationing, especially cruises.

Elaine was a smart lady, but in all their years Cullen had never allowed her to catch on to his extracurricular activities. A simple matter, really. He rose early and headed out of the cabin before she stirred. He enjoyed himself a breakfast buffet, came back to the room, relieved himself of

the previous nights' dinner, and then hurried to be one of

the first to disembark at the port-of-call. Elaine slept

peacefully and Cullen searched the town to select his latest

victim.

In these tropical islands, bars opened early. That's

where he found the best victims. He knew killing tourists

made headlines, and he did not seek publicity, so he let the

tourists and his fellow cruisers live. He stalked the tiny

communities, looking only for unsophisticated locals. He

preferred an alcoholic, a drug addict, a prostitute, a derelict.

It didn't matter whom he killed. Only his power mattered.

He needed to feel their final breaths released from their

bodies. The beauty of his scheme? These tropical islands had

an absence of fancy security cameras around, and usually a

very inept, stone-age police department. The people he

killed were never missed. Even if they were, an American

tourist wouldn't be considered the culprit. On kill days, he wore plain black tee-shirts and shorts. He always wore sunglasses and sometimes a hat which he would dispose of in the water or in a dumpster on his way back to the ship. Cullen had it under control.

Most of the time, he killed in less than one minute. In his mission's early days, he would order a steak dinner the night before a kill day, and steal the knife. How delightfully simple to pick up weapons the cruise lines gave you. They never x-rayed bags leaving a ship, only those brought on board. He ditched knives or whatever weapons in the ocean before he re-boarded, and no one was the wiser. Cullen had heard once that police somewhere pulled his used knife from shallow waters. They had connected the implement to a killing, as it had the name of the cruise line emblazoned on its hilt. That was the closest anyone had ever gotten to considering *any* cruise passenger as a suspect, let alone him.

After that, he'd switched to quick strangulation with his powerful hands and then snapping the victim's neck — difficult until you practiced, but once you got the hang of it, easy as pie.

Cullen's hunger demanded only a single kill per trip, and he stood steady at kill forty-nine after his last cruise. This vacation represented his golden anniversary of sorts. He thought to retire, or at least slow down; however, he could never be sure his inner demons would retire just because he considered the idea. His focus now was simply the number fifty.

CHAPTER TEN

In the eighteen months since Nadif had convinced Dalmar to leave, both men focused their attention on preparing for their next adventure. Convincing Dalmar to run was intensely difficult, but even a bully can be compelled to understand it might be better to run and fight another day than to stand still and die. Nadif's brutally burned face had done the trick. White patches on his dark skin where his eyebrows had been singed off did nothing to improve his physical appeal.

More affected by the burns than he would ever admit, Dalmar shrugged and said, "I have already been working on a new plan." He convinced himself he was moving on to his next mission, rather than running away from a threat. *Aye,* he thought, *pirating working vessels is growing boring. There are bigger — much bigger — prizes out there.*

Dalmar wanted to acquire wealth. That went without saying. But he lusted after being able to disrupt lives and cause chaos. He strove to inflict pain and to gain fame. What he really coveted was a luxury liner. He could already hear wealthy, over-indulged passengers screaming and those screams would lead inexorably to some large American company forking over a huge ransom from deep pockets. He pretended not to care about what others thought, but he craved knowing that his crew, fellow pirates, embraced his greatness among them. It was truly time to step up his game.

Dalmar had convinced nine of his crew to flee with him. He didn't call it *fleeing*, of course. He dangled a bold adventure before them to make them richer than they ever dreamed and more famous than any pirate that had ever lived. When they vanquished this challenge, they would return home to Somalia as conquering heroes. Dalmar knew he would extract revenge from those that had sent him off, too. A vivid picture stirred his mind — after he conquered the cruise liner, he would return to pirate the pirates. What was theirs would be his.

After Dalmar's reorganization, Nadif stayed and so did one Korfa Osman, who had friends and connections in many ports around the world. Osman was an electronics wiz. He understood the latest in shipboard technology and was an expert navigator. Korfa was as dark black and swarthy as Dalmar, but he stood about eight inches shorter than his captain. He was brazen, calculating, and smart, having spent four years at an American college before returning to his native Somalia.

Four other men, Erasto, Taban, Ghedi, and Kader remained. The four were soldiers, one could say, of the highest order. They were loyal to Dalmar and regarded him as a father figure though he had given them no reason to believe he was anything of the kind. Two women remained with the bunch; Nadina Hanad and Amina Ghaman.

Nadina, with her muscular frame, broad shoulders, and

tightly cropped afro, was tougher than any of the men. From

behind, adversaries frequently mistook her as a man. Nadina

was strongly built, but there was no mistaking the

femininity in the curves of her muscular frame. Her long

brown legs drew lusty attention sometimes, yes, but clearly

defined calf and buttock muscles gave her power that

surprised. She chose green military style tank tops cut to

expose the tops of her breasts and generous cleavage, but

whenever she caught one of the men looking at her chest,

she would laugh mockingly.

"You're dreaming, as usual," she would taunt. "If you

ever were so fortunate as to find your ugly self between

these thighs, I'd crush your pelvis like a vise. You'd never be

heard from again."

She'd laugh and thrust out her full lower lip as she thrust her pelvis out and lowered a hand to stroke her thigh.

Whatever man had been caught ogling her charms found himself excited to no end, but he would certainly keep his distance, not completely sure this Amazon meant what she said, but terrified of calling her on it. For a while, even Dalmar kept clear of her for a number of reasons, one of which was he was too busy to confront the arrogant woman.

One afternoon, feeling bored and seeking conquest, Dalmar decided it was time to set her straight. He twisted her tank top in his left fist, and put his knife blade to her throat with his right hand. He then shoved her until she bent over a table, and dragged her cotton shorts to her knees. Stowing his blade in his jeans pocket, he pinned her body with his own powerful legs and raped her from behind.

Grunting, thrusting, he put both hands around her neck, yanking her head up and growling into her ear, "If you want to live you will shout my name. Loud."

She was strong, but not stupid, and less concerned than another woman might be over the assault. No one stopped working, but the crew heard her cries of subservience. From then on, whenever he thought the men might be in need of a morale boost, he took her again — by force and publicly. He knew they respected him more when he so thoroughly dominated a prize they could not hope to take.

The other woman aboard, Amina Ghaman, had found her way into Nadif's bed over the past year and was regarded as his woman. She was a rarity — a college educated Somali girl, so even Dalmar treated her with respect. The captain took her body, of course, but the sex was gentle and loving, discretely done. None of the men, least of all her boyfriend Nadif, suspected Dalmar and

Amina were having sex. Even if Nadif hadn't been oblivious,

he would never have believed a trusted comrade, his

captain, would take his woman behind his back.

Over the course of several months Dalmar's pirates

traveled from Somalia over land through Kenya, then to

Tanzania. From Tanzania they crossed Zambia and then left

Africa, via Angola. From Angola they flew to Puerto La

Cruz, Venezuela. There they purchased weapons and

acquired a boat which they would sail east to the Caribbean.

Dalmar briefed his crew, describing basics of the plan.

They would each be assigned specific jobs and each must

perform their responsibilities to perfection if the mission

were to succeed. He told them their target, a luxury liner

filled with rich Americans and wealthy foreign nationals,

belonged to an American company. Dalmar already had

people on the inside willing to help.

"We're after high ransoms on dozens of passengers as well as tills from the busy casino. Passengers carry all manner of valuables on board, too. Rest assured the ship's owners will lay down a huge sum for its safe return. This voyage will be worth your time and effort to do it right," he admonished the pirates, male and female. Dalmar guessed at least some of his crew would fail to return, but he figured that was a detail they didn't need to know.

Dalmar had considered several ships as targets, but knowing he'd have inside help on the *Treasure of the Seas* clinched his decision. He needed someone with working knowledge of ship systems and procedures, someone who knew what sort of security lapses might occur. Dalmar needed someone disgruntled or in tight financial straits — Korfa Osman's friend was the troubled Chief Security Officer, Drago Stevinski, on *the Treasure of the Seas*. Dalmar grinned to himself as he worked on details. *I must live right,*

he mused.

CHAPTER ELEVEN

As soon as their bags were unpacked and clothes put away, the Sampson family set out to explore the wonder that was *the Treasure of the Seas*. They walked forward to the first stairwell they could find and decided to head topside first. Jen had a printout of the ship's layout she'd brought from home, but it was quickly abandoned so they could keep up with Robby taking two steps at a time on his way to anywhere. On deck ten, the upbeat sounds of a steel band drew Joanne and company to where an elaborate barbeque grill sent the smell of hamburgers, hot dogs, and chicken wafting through the air.

Jen turned to her mom, trying to outshout the music, "Could it get more relaxing than this?"

Joanne yelled back, "I could definitely get used to this, you know!" They both laughed when they saw Robby coming toward them with a hamburger in one hand and a plate piled high with French fries in the other.

"Thanks for the fries, little bro, did you get any for yourself?" Jen said as she swiped a few fries from his plate.

"Hey, no way," Robby exclaimed, slapping her hand when it returned for a second theft. "It's every cruiser for himself!"

"Oh come on just a couple — I don't feel like getting on line."

"I didn't get on line. I just grabbed a plate and Mr. Nickels let me cut him."

As they wrangled, Cullen Nickels walked up to them with a plate piled high with burgers and fries. He said, "Ladies, Robby has already figured things out. Please, accept these burgers as a welcome aboard gift. From here on though, you're on your own."

"Why, thank you sir, don't mind if we do," said Joanne. "As long as you join us."

"I'd love to — but please, call me Cullen. And Robby, you can call me Cullen, or Mr. Cullen, if your mom prefers, but I'd rather not go by Mr. Nickels."

Joanne took Cullen's cold hand in hers, "I'm sorry we didn't introduce ourselves before, I'm Joanne, and this is my daughter Jennifer. You've already started a relationship with Robby."

Jen cut in, "She'd like to be called *Jo* this week, if you don't mind."

"Oh stop," said Jo, tapping her daughter's wrist. "*Jo* will be fine. Cullen, what happened to your wife?"

"She's not the sociable type. I like to get out and meet new people, but she likes to do a little relaxing, and oh, a lot of gambling."

Jen did the thumb-to-the-mouth gesture and threw her head back. Cullen roared with laughter while Jo slapped her daughter's shoulder this time.

"And a whole lot of that," he agreed. "You've got some sharp kids there, Jo."

They realized Robby was gone again and after a brief panic they saw him walking through the crowd. This time, he carried a hunk of twirled chocolate ice cream that looked like the Leaning Tower of Pisa would if it were balanced on a waffle cone. The boy held the cone in one hand while trying to keep it from falling with the other. Every few steps he took a lick. Most of the ice cream ended up on his lips and nose.

"Boy, this kid's serious about this, isn't he" marveled Cullen.

Jo started to scold Robby about ruining his appetite, but something inside clicked out of mother-mode and into vacation-mode. *So he ruins his dinner, this week is a once in a lifetime thing.*

****

A few hours later, finished exploring, the Sampson's dressed and set on their way to the Captain's dinner table. Robby wore a Hawaiian shirt and a sailor's cap given him by a friend, Jen looked hip and nautical in white jeans and a blue and white horizontally striped top, and Jo had chosen a short, white linen skirt and a bright yellow sleeveless top. At the last minute, she'd tucked a white flower in her hair. She stuck her room key into her tiny evening clutch and herded her brood out the door.

We look marvelous, she thought, and she snapped several pictures of them along the way to dinner, stopping more than once to ask another passenger if he or she wouldn't mind taking a picture of all three of them. Arriving at the table they found Captain Fredrickson already seated and engaged in conversation with two other officers. The men stopped talking and rose when the family approached.

"So glad you could all make it," the Captain said, extending his hand to Jo and smiling at all three. "I'd like to introduce you to two of my finest officers. This is Giovanna Stelina from Italy. He's our Chief Purser. Drago Stevinski is our Chief Security Officer on board. He hails from Bulgaria."

They shook hands all around and exchanged pleasantries. The wine steward stepped up and tipped a portion of pale gold liquid into the captain's glass. Seated again, Gunnar sipped and nodded acceptance. He turned to Jo.

"I've chosen a sweet Riesling from Germany. Do you know anything about wines?"

"No, not really," said Jo. "I'll be happy with whatever you chose."

"Good, because I know nothing about them myself. They always bring me the sweet Riesling from Germany, and I always tell them it's great."

The group laughed and Jo thought, *what an interesting man, and what an interesting life he must have had to get to where he is.* She imagined him as the commander of Navy ships and guessed he'd been to war zones and fought battles regular citizens never heard about. She couldn't have been further from the truth, but she found herself at least mildly attracted to him and the exotic images she had conjured. Cullen Nickels and his wife paused on the way to their own table.

"What's this?" Cullen said, shaking his head, "I've been on, like, thirty-five of these cruises and I've never had dinner with the captain. Must be nice!" Cullen and Captain Fredrickson acknowledged each other; warily it seemed to Jen, in that way when men instantly decide they dislike each other but pretend to be friendly. After the awkward pause Cullen steered his wife toward their own table.

They dined first on shrimp cocktail, followed by a creamy tomato soup finished with a dollop of sour cream and a sprig of fresh cilantro. Then came spinach salad topped with walnuts and dates, and that preceded roast prime rib au jus with horseradish cream. They enjoyed everything, but about half way through the prime rib, Robby began to sweat and his face turned pale.

"Your boy there is quite the good little eater, for an eight year old," Drago observed.

Robby smiled and raised his lemonade glass in agreement. Jo shook her head in rueful surprise. "Trust me; at home he only eats hot dogs and pizza."

Robby jumped in, "Hey I didn't get to have any pizza yet. That's the first thing on my list for…"

He burped, then lunged sideways and spewed

everything he'd eaten all day onto Drago Stevinski's lap.

CHAPTER TWELVE

While *Treasure of the Seas* passengers enjoyed the festive first evening of their cruise, Abdi Dalmar and his crew were on the Island of St. Thomas, finalizing their plans. St. Thomas would be the cruise's first stop, followed by the company's private island of OAR Cay. *Treasure of the Seas* was two days away from reaching their first port of call.

Because OAR was still in the process of building a new dock, large enough to accommodate their ships, *the Treasure of the Seas* would anchor off shore and use two tenders to ferry passengers ashore to OAR Cay and back. It was a one-day stop, meaning passengers must return to the ship by five p.m. For the ride back, they would be picked up where they had been dropped earlier in the day. The tenders would start shuttling passengers at nine in the morning and run back and forth continuously throughout the day, allowing passengers to come and go to the island as many

times as they liked.

Dalmar intended to have one tender loaded with

weapons and waiting for his crew. They'd sail from the

island to the ship alone. Korfa Osman's security friend had

already made fake identification badges for the crew, but

that was a backup; the friend planned on being the officer

stationed at the entrance to the ship when the pirates

arrived. Once aboard, they would deploy to key areas and

take the ship by force. Korfa's buddy would summon all

security to the entry point, where they would assemble and

be hurled into the sea. Then the nine pirates, plus Korfa's

friend and one other inside accomplice, would fan out in

wider directions to eliminate the crew and split up

passengers remaining aboard.

The plan called for Dalmar's men to split into teams.

Erasto and Taban would take the two lower decks, gather

crew and staff, and lock them in a conference room. The two

pirates were to work their way up the ship to help on other

decks. The other inside accomplice was a meek Croatian girl,

named Doratai. She worked in guest relations and would be

in charge of producing critically important guest and worker

logs to let Dalmar know exactly how many crew and

passengers remained on ship. The plan called for Ghadi and

Kader to work from deck three up to seven, clearing

passengers and crew. The tuff as nails Nadina Hanad would

start at deck eight and work her way up on her own. Korfa

Osman, Nadif, and Amina would head to the bridge to team

with Korfa's security friend and commandeer control of the

vessel. Remaining crew would be held at gunpoint and

made to steer the ship into open waters. Amina, because she

spoke several languages, was in charge of making

announcements, calmly directing remaining guests to three

designated areas where they would remain until Dalmar

was sure everyone was accounted for. The pirates would

cross check logs, and only when they had a handle on the

number of people on the ship, would they proceed.

Dalmar's conspirators would dress in white sailing

uniforms like the crew wore, so guests wouldn't panic at

seeing strangers around. The goal was to get everyone

where they wanted them in an orderly fashion. Amina's

announcements would direct passengers, but also promise a

special gift of a free future cruise, courtesy of OAR. The crew

would hear similar promises of cash bonuses. To Abdi

Dalmar, the plan seemed elaborate yet simple; he knew

enough about human nature to expect glitches. Dalmar

cared nothing about odds — he knew his own skills, he

prepared as carefully as always, and his attention to detail

would sway the odds in his favor.

CHAPTER THIRTEEN

Robby spent most of his first evening aboard *the Treasure of the Seas* with his head in the commode. When his head wasn't in the toilet, his mother soothed him with cold compresses made by wrapping a small towel around ice. In the middle of the night, a cleanup crew came to the Sampson's room and washed down the walls of the cabin; they could take no chance that something other than overeating had caused his vomiting. Cruise ships in general had become more and more sensitive over the years to a single virus causing a slew of miserably sick passengers. Miserably sick passengers didn't buy alcohol and they didn't go to casinos and they asked for their money back for expensive shore excursions they'd already purchased, from which the cruise lines took a generous cut. Miserably sick passengers also caused other passengers to become miserably sick, and then they all went home and blogged about it or wrote scathingly bad reviews about the line's cleanliness, or lack thereof, and what a horrible vacation they'd had. That, in turn, led to tawdry reputations, deserved or not, handed out by people who may not have ever been on an OAR ship.

Captain Gunnar, spurred by his interest in Jo and his usual concern for his passengers, paid a personal visit right after midnight. He was not in uniform but had donned a pair of Khaki shorts and an Izod pullover. He wore sandals with no socks and carried a bag of ship's goodies he'd purchased earlier at a discount, with his own money, from one of the gift shops. He waited until the cleanup crew left and then tapped on the semi-open cabin door.

"Just wanted to see how our little sailor is doing," he said by way of announcing himself.

Jo jumped up and reflexively re-tightened the belt of the ship robe she wore. She stepped to the door and held out a hand to Gunnar.

"He seems a bit better — no more throwing up, but that might be because he's got nothing left in him."

"Probably," Gunnar agreed. "I've asked the ship's doctor to pay him a visit, kind of off the record. You won't have to worry about filling out insurance forms or paying for anything."

"Thank you, Captain, you're more than kind. We appreciate everything."

Jen cut in, "Captain are we quarantined? I mean there's no way I'm going to stay in this cabin for seven days. I'll go batty!"

"No, not at all. You're free to go out to the teen club right now, if you'd like," he replied. He recognized his comment as a lame attempt to get the girl out of the room so he could spend time talking with her mother. He also figured Jen was perceptive enough to pick up on that. His motive bothered him, so he decided to correct his behavior.

"But it might be best if you stayed in for tonight; these things usually run their course in about twenty-four hours, probably less time in someone Robby's age. Tomorrow we have a full day at sea and I'll assign one of our children's attendants to stay with Robby so the two of you can have some fun. How's that sound?"

"Works for me," said Jen. "I'm tired anyway."

"That's really not necessary Captain, but thank you," Jo added.

"I insist," he said. "I'll have someone here at eight-thirty sharp so you can go for breakfast. That's Captain's orders, and the last time I checked I was still in command of this ship." He turned to look directly at Jo and continued, "If

I may be so bold, I would ask that you join me for lunch tomorrow in my cabin."

"A Captain's order as well?" Jo teased.

"No, ma'am, that is a Captain's respectful request, and by the law of the sea it can be refused. Of course, I can make you walk the plank, if it pleases me."

Jo giggled like a school girl, "Is there still such a thing as walking the plank? I thought that went out with old pirate movies."

CHAPTER FOURTEEN

First full day at sea — sailing day.

As promised, promptly at eight-thirty a.m. someone knocked at cabin 9500. By then, Jo and Jen had showered and shared their hair dryer, so they were ready to head out the door. Robby seemed slightly better, but a bit groggy. Jo explained to him that Penny, from Great Britain, was a children's counselor, and would be staying with him while she and Jen went to breakfast. He rolled over sluggishly and closed his eyes. As they walked out the door, Robby sat up in the bed; eyes still shut, and said, "Mom, can I have pizza today?"

Jo and Jen sat down in the main dining room and tried to map out their day. Jen ordered grapefruit juice, egg-battered French toast, and a side order of bacon. Jo decided on half a grapefruit, two poached eggs with sausage, and coffee. They shared a bagel with cream cheese and smoked salmon, declaring they would eat heartily in honor of poor Robby. Relaxed and comfortable, they giggled like sisters.

"So what do you think of him mom?" Jen asked.

"Think of whom?"

"You know what I mean. I don't think a ship's captain normally pays this much attention to any guests. I'm sure most never even get to see him."

"Well, I'm not sure," replied Jo.

"What? You're not sure what you think of him, or you're not sure about guests getting to see the captain?"

"You know, I'm just not sure. It's been a long time since anyone's paid attention to me and now, all of a sudden, I've got the Captain of the cruise hitting on me. Guess I'm creeped out a little."

"I don't want to put a damper on anything, but be careful," Jen said. "I've read lots of stories about people who work on cruise ships taking; you know, um — *advantage* of women passengers and stuff."

"Oh, come on now, I'm not going to sleep with anybody, if that's what you're worried about. He simply asked me to lunch in his cabin."

Mother and daughter paused, shared a long, knowing look, and burst out laughing together.

"I'm going to have sex, aren't I? I'd better wear my pretty underwear," Jo said, deadpan.

Jen's eyes popped and she wrinkled up her face. "Ewww. Mom, don't just come right out and say it. If it was me plotting this, you'd flip out at me going to some stranger's room and hooking up!" She realized her mom was pulling her leg. "Yeah, even if the stranger was tall and handsome and wearing a uniform and commanding one of the largest ships afloat."

Another burst of laughter caused some fellow-passengers to glance over and smile. Jo cherished the mother-daughter moment and realized that most moms could never talk like this with their teenage girls. However, she had her boundaries.

"Look, let's put this hooking up and sex talk to bed for now," Jo said grinning at her own pun. She slurped her coffee. "I'll take it slow and see where it leads."

"Fine. But so far, my brother has been puking his brains out, landed himself in quasi-quarantine and it looks like my mom is gonna boink the captain. What can happen next?"

****

Cullen Nickels sat on the Lido deck working at his second breakfast.

Earlier, he'd been to the dining room where he shared breakfast with a table of strangers and enjoyed smoked salmon on a bagel with cream cheese and capers.

He'd been amused by the southern folks at the table who'd

asked him what those little green things he was putting on

his bagel were. While he was explaining to someone that

capers were the bud of a plant, one of the men asked in a

distinctly Texas accent, "Now is that thar salmon fish on that

bagel yur eatin' raw, or whut?" The fellow pronounced the

"L" in *salmon.*

Cullen stared down his new opponent and swallowed

the bite he had taken.

"No. Actually, it's cooked in a refrigerator for a few

days and treated, if you will. Not cooked in the sense that

you would put something on a fry pan, but technically it is

cooked, not raw."

Puzzled, the man looked at Cullen for a moment

before he spoke again, "Is it like that sushi crap? Cause I

don't eat nuthin' that was swimmin' around a few minutes

before, if you get my drift." He looked around the table and grinned, happily encouraging others to laugh with him.

"Would you try a bite of it if I handed you this hundred dollar bill for your troubles?" Cullen asked — his color was rising so that his ears were tinged slightly red. He spoke softly.

Everyone at the table stopped their conversations and regarded the money Cullen had slapped down in front of them. "It's just that every man has his price," Cullen continued. "What's yours? Is it one-hundred? A thousand? What will it take for you to put this filthy piece of raw fish in your mouth, as opposed to that hunk of sausage you're eating? That came from a pig's ass, you know?"

Cullen liked toying with the idiot, but, sensed unease at the table. He picked up his money and laughed.

"Just joking with you. I don't like the stuff either; I'm trying it for the first time, myself." Those at the table chortled appreciation.

Cullen's second breakfast, on the Lido deck, consisted of very dry scrambled eggs with cottage cheese, grits, and a soft roll. He had a sudden desire for pig, so he piled sausage and bacon on his plate. He jammed some of it onto the roll with the eggs and made himself a sandwich which he consumed with orange juice and a cup of decaf.

As he ate, he gazed out the window, watching the sea swirl by. It was a gorgeous day for sailing, and an even more gorgeous day for contemplating tomorrow's kill. This kind of moment kept him cruising and killing. Life was most enjoyable when he was alone with his thoughts, looking out over the ocean, remembering his past kills, and visualizing his next one.

Tomorrow they would be in St. Thomas where he had been three times before and where he had killed twice. Once was no problem. Twice was happenstance. But a third kill in the same place, even if separated by many years? Someone might put those together as a pattern. Cullen didn't like patterns. Even unsophisticated police departments could link tiny clues from crimes nowadays, and technically St. Thomas was American soil, so, although they would probably rather not, American mainland authorities had jurisdiction to get involved in something they deemed worthy of their time. That's why he knew a third kill on the island was pushing the envelope. Cullen knew the risks, but he loved St. Thomas and the urge was undeniable. He would retire St. Thomas as a kill zone after tomorrow.

From the last trip to St. Thomas, he remembered he could see Havensight Dockside Shopping Mall from his cabin balcony. A series of small jewelry, clothing, and liquor shops, it faced docked ships and so it was the first place every passenger went when they disembarked. Since it numbered among the busiest places on the island it would not provide the cover he needed. However, just beyond the mall and up the mountainside stood a large tin building called the Al Coheri Liquor Mall. Amused, he remembered the liquor sign with a smaller sign attached that read, *Also Serving Pizza*. Locals would do anything to attract American tourists, including serving up lousy frozen pizza in a liquor store.

Beyond the Al Coheri, a bit to the left and slightly further up the mountainside, sat a small bar — Razzy's. It was a rundown place where locals hung out and it was perfect for tomorrow's festivities. Cullen would arrive early, settling down to hang out in the bar all day. He would bring a newspaper to spread out across the table, pretending to read until just the right victim made an appearance. He was nothing if not a patient man. Watching and contemplating and fantasizing about his victim infused him with some of the pleasure he gleaned from his hobby. He had gotten so good at this dance that pre-planning and picking the right victim provided almost as much thrill as did the killing itself. Always, he risked the possibility of being captured or of somebody witnessing the kill. If he was seen in the act, he planned to walk toward the main mall and disappear into a preselected clothing shop. There, he would purchase a new shirt and a hat; make a quick change in the store dressing room, and then casually walk back to the ship. He figured authorities would be inclined to suspect a local first; after all, most murder victims know their attackers. Who would ever think a tourist would venture into a bar to kill a local stranger? Tourists were attracted to the liquor and pizza, not to chaos and mayhem.

That last time in St. Thomas, Cullen had had one of

his closest calls to date. He'd used a rusty pocket knife he'd

found earlier in the day to kill his drunken victim. When he

tried to slit the guy's throat, Cullen had to apply way more

force than usual, and the man spurted blood onto Cullen's

shirt. Finishing the drunk off with a quick snapping of the

neck, Cullen sprinted around a corner, but his getaway

shook him to the core. He had run directly into a female

police officer. She was a bicycle patrol woman wearing a

white helmet and dressed in blue shorts with a blue-collared

shirt that had POLICE in large yellow print across the back.

He knew that even if he pretended to have witnessed the

crime he'd just committed, his name would go into a file and

suspicions could be raised. Thinking fast, he purposely

tripped over his own feet and fell face first into a mud

puddle. The police officer turned, startled to see a muddy

tourist with blood coursing down his leg and pooling into his shoe.

"I'm so sorry, officer." He remembered blathering and grabbing his injured leg, "I'm such a klutz. I've got to get back to my ship and get this looked at. My God, it hurts!"

He declined her offer of assistance and gave the name of a different ship, also in port at the time, then kept walking, refusing to give in to his urge to look back. When he thought he was clear, he ducked into a clothing store, picked out the loudest Hawaiian shirt he could find and headed for the changing room to clean up his knee and don the shirt. Leaving the shop, he strolled casually back to the ship, greeting as many people as possible as he re-boarded. When the cruise ended and Cullen returned home a few days later, he searched the Internet and newspapers for any reports about his victim. He could only find one story and no follow ups. The local newspaper had said:

An unidentified St. Thomas man was found beaten and stabbed to death about one block east of the Havensight Dockside Mall on Tuesday. The man was an apparent victim of gang violence plaguing the area in recent weeks. Police said several area gangs have been holding initiations in which recruits must beat or kill a victim to gain membership. Police have no identity for the victim, but are holding two suspects in custody. According to police sources, both have confessed to the crime.

A narrow escape. He lucked out because people too chicken to actually murder someone claimed his kill so they could gain entrance to a street gang. *Bet that gang would love to have me in it,* he thought, preening. However, he had learned a serious lesson, and stabbings, as much as they excited him, were deemed too risky. He retired them from his arsenal.

On the *Treasure of the Seas*, at exactly twelve-thirty p.m. a staff member arrived outside room 9500 to escort Jo to the captain's cabin for lunch. She wore her Victoria's Secret underwear.

CHAPTER FIFTEEN

Dalmar and his crew stayed at Chari Azar's home on St. Thomas. He was an acquaintance of Korfa's, and they promised to pay him one-hundred thousand American dollars to house them for the night and then put their equipment onto one of his boats. The OAR Company also paid Azar for the use of his two boats to ferry passengers to and from the anchored ship. He was an independent contractor slated to be laid off in three months. OAR had purchased a shuttle craft designed to be more gas efficient and to carry bigger loads of passengers on each trip. Azar provided employment for a group of islanders consisting of himself and his crew: Azar's wife and his two sons, plus a local guy that needed cash to support his drug habit — he subbed when a member of the family couldn't make it to work. OAR hadn't even offered them a chance to crew the new shuttles. This family supported part of the local economy and it would be going away with no warning or respect. Azar qualified as disgruntled.

When the pirates arrived, Dalmar handed Chari Azar a briefcase filled with cash then walked with Chari as he took the case into his bedroom and opened it. Chari peeked inside and closed the case without counting. He placed it in a closet, unaware that Dalmar took note of that placement. Dalmar would seek to reclaim it the next day.

The crew split up into two guest bedrooms and went over their roles in tomorrow's plot. Dalmar sat on a barstool in the kitchen, drinking rum from a glass marked with a faded American sports team logo. He eyeballed a picture on the wall of Chari's older son, Ani, playing soccer, and then turned as he heard the twenty year-old walk into the room.

"You are a player of futbol?" he asked. "Are you any good?"

"I am. I was one of the best on the island."

Dalmar mocked, "The best on the island of St. Thomas? You must be terrible. I can't imagine your competition." He continued to laugh and the young man tensed.

"And where did you play your futbol, sir?"

"I, child, played in my prime for the Somali National team."

Now it was Ani's turn to laugh.

"You scoff at me? Really? The Somali National team? How many World Cups did you participate in?" he asked, knowing full well that Somali's National team had never made it to the World Cup.

Silent, Dalmar took a gulp of his drink.

Ani sized him up. "Let's go out and play," he said, "For my father's life."

Dalmar could hear that the kid wasn't joking and he turned his head slightly to regard the boy.

"What are you asking me for, young man?"

"I am not the fool my father is. I don't know your plans, but I know whatever you paid my father, he will not live to spend it. If I prove myself better than you, you let my family go with no questions asked. I can assure you of our silence."

Dalmar stood up, putting his full intimidating frame in front of the young man.

"And how will you do that? The police will trace the boats directly to you and, as soon as they pull out your first fingernail, you will all tell them exactly who we are and where to find us."

"If I lose, you can have my life," the boy said, trying to hold back a tear forming in his left eye as he stood facing Dalmar toe-to-toe.

The pirate paused, considering. "You give me a scenario in which I am not the victor in either case. You should feel lucky I don't slaughter you all right now. Be glad I shall at least let you enjoy this last night together as a family." He turned his back to the boy and paced for a moment.

"On the other hand," he said, turning back and glaring, "it is lucky for you I like you — you remind me of myself as a youth. So, my proposition is this: You will kill your father so your brother and mother shall live. Then you will stay aboard the shuttle as our driver while my crew and I board *the Treasure of the Seas*."

The boy shook his head. I will be your sitting duck."

Dalmar grabbed the boy's head playfully, but with tremendous force, putting him in a headlock. "You will have to take your chances. You are not in a position to be anything *but* a sitting duck," he said, laughing without a trace of humor.

On his way to the bedroom that housed his two female crew members, Dalmar passed the room where the men were resting and smoking. None were asleep. In their minds, they went over and over all the possibilities for the next day. He entered his target room and asked Nadina and Amina if they were comfortable. They each nodded in his direction, surprised by the apparent concern.

"I am not," he announced.

He slid his zipper down and dropped his pants. "I am in need of some soothing attention."

As things heated up in that room, Nadif rose; hearing moans and sighs through the thin walls. Through the partially open door of Nadina and Amina's room, he watched Nadina stroking Dalmar's back with her bare breasts. Amina sat on Dalmar's lap facing him; her head tilted back, eyes closed, as the pirate leader cupped her breasts, roughly pinching the hardened buds of her nipples.

CHAPTER SIXTEEN

Jo had expected her escort to lead her all the way downstairs to the lower decks where she believed the Captain's cabin would be. Instead, they stopped on deck seven and went forward. She was taken to the entrance of Sashimi, the ships' Sushi bar. It appeared to be closed, but inside Captain Gunnar waited at the bar, with the sushi chef working busily behind him.

"I hope you don't mind the change of plans," he said. "And I hope you're a fan of sushi."

"I am," she said, not acknowledging the first part of his statement.

"It's just that you can never be too careful these days with perceptions. I'm sorry, but my job takes precedence over any personal feelings I might have."

Jo nodded, finding herself interested in his admission of some sort of personal feelings. *For her?*

"It's important you understand that I intend to enjoy your company, while also enjoying some of the finest sushi at sea." He nodded to the chef who instantly began carving up a perfect piece of tuna.

It hit Jo that Gunnar might have done some research on her background and figured out she worked for a television station. It didn't matter that she wasn't a reporter who investigated improprieties like those on the Captain's mind; it mattered that she worked in the media. She figured if she were a janitor at the station, he would probably have reacted in the same manner. Everyone worried about the hidden camera that would bring them down, and Captain Gunnar Fredrickson apparently felt the same way.

"Captain Gunnar, may I speak bluntly?" she asked.

He nodded, smiling a careful smile.

"It occurs to me that you may have snooped into my profession and might feel a bit nervous about it. I assure you, I have no hidden cameras or hidden agendas. You and your cruise line are not a story to me, if that's what you're worried about. On the one hand, I'm flattered you've taken time to research me. On the other, I'm worried that you took the time to research me, as opposed to — oh I don't know — maybe steering the boat," she finished wryly. She smiled at his astonished face and realized she'd called him out.

"Bravo," he said. "You win. It's true — one can never be too careful. Truth is, I've never had lunch with a passenger in the manner I wanted to with you, and suddenly I saw every possible misperception."

"Well, let's just get this straight then," she said, looking him directly in the eye and holding her gaze steady, "I don't personally give a shit about any possible misperceptions. Now, let's eat sushi."

The sushi chef had stopped working so he could listen to the conversation, and now he made a show of bustling about. He laid the first dish in front of them. Eying

each other, Jo and Gunnar laughed under their breath as

they tasted the delicate rolls.

"How long have you worked in television?" he said.

"How long have you been driving ships?" she said at

the same time.

****

Cullen paced the deck for several hours, deep in

thought. Like a great athlete preparing for a big game, he

visualized his conquests. He needed to see his victory going

perfectly in his mind. As he walked he looked for potential

murder weapons, remembering that he had once used a

rolled up magazine. He had watched a martial arts

instructor show how you could kill a man by striking him

correctly, the full force of the magazine thrust into his nose.

This worked better in theory than in reality. Cullen had

struck a man with a magazine, but it had only stunned the

guy and he'd had had to finish him off with good old ingenuity. First Cullen had used his shoe to knock the victim cold, and then he'd finished the job by shoving a thick candy bar, still in its wrapper, down the victims' throat. Good thing he'd had a back-up that day, and a desire for a Snickers bar. He still loved the concept of unrolling the magazine and tossing it into the trash. It was the perfect way to dispose of a murder weapon. So into the trash went the magazine and then the candy bar wrapper after he'd eaten its contents.

Another time, he'd removed the shoelace from a shoe left outside a children's play area. He went into town and strangled a prostitute with it. He returned to the play area to find the shoe hadn't been touched, so he casually laced it up in perfect alignment. Then, he walked away. Later Cullen fantasized about the boy returning to school — the shoelace talked to all the other kids' shoelaces, telling them what it had done on its vacation.

****

Jen spent part of her afternoon sunning by the pool and reading. She tried her hand at the rock climbing wall and spent some time in one of the ships many hot tubs, abandoning that endeavor when an overweight, over-hairy man lumbered in and sloshed down next to her. Jen laughed when a little boy, standing on the deck while his mother was in the tub, innocently queried, "Mommy, why does that man have boobies?"

She wandered away, sampled some pizza, and then grabbed a bowl of Mongolian barbeque cooked on large woks by chefs in oriental robes and headgear. To her, the chefs looked Japanese, but then again, she wasn't sure what proper Mongolian dress should look like.

After lunch, she decided that if her mom could boink the Captain, Jen should certainly be entitled to a full body massage, no questions asked. So she headed up to the spa on deck thirteen and indulged herself in a full treatment

massage which she charged to her mother's account. The

massage made her body feel better than it ever had. She felt

her leg muscles, although temporarily weakened by the

deep relaxation, were now stronger than ever. Even her

fingers and toes got a workout. She left with a sense of body-

confidence she couldn't remember having before.

Relaxed and happy, Jen decided to peruse the mall

shops. On the way, she grabbed a slice of spinach and feta

pizza, promising herself she would go soon to check on

Robby. She admired some watches, and then tried a few

spritzes of different fragrances. As she moved on, a

glistening silver necklace caught her eye. It had a heart in its

center, with the word *Love* split apart and cradling the heart.

Jen was not in love, had never been, in fact, yet the sheer

beauty of the necklace made it something she suddenly *had*

to have. A clerk approached her, smiling and nodding.

"That's gorgeous, isn't it?" the clerk said. Jen nodded

and the clerk took the necklace out of the case to show it to

her. He looped the chain around his hand and held the heart

against her throat.

Jen would have sworn she felt some sort of power

from the necklace when it touched her skin; she also felt the

strongest desire she'd ever had to own something. She could

explain away the massage purchase to her mother, but

adding this expensive necklace to the bill would be going

over the top. Still, she had to have it. Without further

thought to consequences, she fastened the necklace on, and

when the clerk turned away for a split second, Jen turned

abruptly and smoothly made her way out the door, her heart

pounding.

CHAPTER SEVENTEEN

Captain Gunnar and Jo talked for hours, though it seemed like only minutes had passed. After leaving the sushi bar, he took her on a quick tour of the kitchen and then showed her the ship's bridge. He so wanted to take her to his quarters, but he resisted. She wanted to go but made no attempt to persuade him. They realized that what they wanted was not going to happen, so they enjoyed as much of the day as they could before the Captain was called back to the bridge. He thought about giving her a peck on the cheek. Instead, he put his left hand on her shoulder to keep her at bay and then extended his right hand for a shake. It was a disappointing end to a wonderful day, but they both understood why it had to be that way.

When Jo got back to the cabin she was surprised to see Jen taking care of Robby. Jen had gotten back a few minutes earlier and dismissed Penny. Though Robby was still feeling queasy, he begged for pizza again. The women decided it would be best for them to eat in the cabin, and they called room service. It was a chicken sandwich and fries for Jen, pasta primavera for Jo, and warm chicken broth, not pizza, for Robby.

It was about eight in the evening when they finished their meal. Deciding to watch an in-room movie, they switched on the television and settled in. Though they had originally planned to go to the beach when they arrived in St. Thomas the next day, their plans were up in the air at this point. Half an hour into the movie, mom and daughter both giggled out loud, realizing the preposterousness of sitting in a tiny cabin while nightlife buzzed all around them. They'd traveled far to hang out in a room smaller than their living room, watching a screen that could fit five times over into their big one at home.

"Let's take turns tomorrow going off the ship," Jen said. "You can go in the morning and do some shopping, and then I'll head for the beach in the afternoon."

Jo recognized the offer as an example of her daughter attempting to grow up, right in front of her. She felt pride and a gentle sense of impending loss.

"Listen," Jo said, "I really don't like the idea of you going off by yourself in a strange place." She hesitated and then looked her daughter directly in her eyes. "But, you've never given me a single reason not to trust you. You've always been responsible and I'm going to allow you your freedom. Tomorrow the day is yours to do as you please. I'll stay with Robby."

Jen tried not to look as over-excited as she felt. She also tried not to look as guilty as she knew she was.

****

Elaine Nickels had spent most of her first day at sea playing video poker. At one point, she was up more than four-hundred dollars but finished with winnings of exactly ninety-five dollars. She was happy with her day, but considering the amount of drinks she'd consumed, she figured her winnings were closer to twenty bucks.

Cullen spent time doing an aerobics class in the gym then took a dip in the pool. He ate lunch in the dining room and again at the buffet. He observed an art auction and caught a towel-folding demonstration. He grabbed a little sushi at Sashimi and then headed back to the cabin to dress for dinner, all the while admiring his capacity for excess.

Husband and wife left arm in arm for the dining room at about five minutes to six and were seated at their table a few minutes later. Dinner was fabulous, but Cullen ate almost none of it. Elaine ate like a horse. He asked what her plans were for tomorrow's stop in St. Thomas.

"I've scheduled an eleven o' clock seaweed massage. I figured I'll play a little bingo in the afternoon. What about you, dear?"

"Oh, the usual, find a bar and observe the locals. Enjoy the tropical breeze through what's left of my hair."

They laughed together and she took a swig of her wine, stared at the glass, and spoke without looking up. "Don't get into any trouble, dear. You know I couldn't get along without you."

CHAPTER EIGHTEEN

At exactly eight a.m., Captain Gunnar steered *the Treasure of the Seas* into port at St. Thomas. Three other cruise ships were already anchored. The weather was perfect; sunny and bright with a cool tropical breeze that swayed the palms gently. Cullen had eaten breakfast and was on the balcony of his cabin having his third cup of coffee. Earlier he had clipped, removed, and placed in his pocket, the cord used to hang wet clothes across the shower in the bathroom. It was today's murder weapon of choice. He'd used that technique once before on the island of Turks and Caicos, and it proved reliable. The cord was strong enough not to snap and elastic enough to pull tightly around someone's neck. With any luck, it might be two or three cruises from now when it was discovered missing.

He waited now with a killers' cool anticipation. He was a hunter poised in a tree, anticipating a deer coming into his sights. He could see the Havensight Dockside shopping mall. Then the Al Coheri Liquor Mall came into view. Just out of sight lay the place where, later today, he would make his fiftieth kill. He felt his pants move and his insides stir. He stood and walked out of the cabin with a zombie-like focus, while his dear wife, pretending to be asleep, dripped a tear into her pillow.

****

Jo and Jen called room service again at breakfast and ordered bagels and salmon with cream cheese, along with an omelet to share — cheddar cheese plus bacon, green peppers, onions, and ham. Sipping coffee, they chatted about how much they'd been eating, and then, for the first time on the trip, Jen mentioned her dad.

"That was almost as good as the omelets dad used to make." She caught herself, but too late. "I mean," she paused to gather her thoughts, "don't you miss him? I mean dad really shined on family vacations."

Jo stroked her daughters' hair and gave an unexpected answer.

"Yes, I miss him. He was my guiding light. He was everything. It just ended. It was time to move on and make new lives for ourselves."

"But mom, whatever happened to staying together for the family? Why couldn't you wait until Robby went off to college or something?"

Jo had no reply. Jen realized she had made her mother uncomfortable, and that was one thing she didn't want to do before leaving on her own today. She aimed for humor, "So what am I gonna call this guy, Captain Daddy, or what?"

****

Dalmar's crew awoke to the screams of Chari Azar's wife. Her son Ani stood over her husband's lifeless body. Ani had stabbed his sleeping father several times in the chest and blood soaked the bed.

"Why Ani? Why?" she screamed, pounding her son's chest with her fists.

Ani, still firmly gripping the knife in his right hand, walked to the closet where the briefcase full of money had been placed the day before. He picked the satchel up with his left hand, and walked to the doorway.

"Get up and get out of here," he ordered his mother. "Get my brother and leave now. Do not come back here again."

Dalmar and the rest of his crew appeared in the narrow hallway.

"Get out, now!" the young man repeated as he placed himself and his knife between Dalmar and his mother. She stood immobilized, looking at her son as he thrust the briefcase against her limp hand. Holding the blade in his teeth for a moment, he grabbed her hand, and forced the case into it, then shoved her, not roughly but firmly.

"You go now, mamma, and do not look back. I'm with *him* now," he said, jerking a thumb at Dalmar.

Dalmar had had every intention of taking the money back, it was his; but for some reason, he took a step backward and nodded to the mother and then to Ani. The woman grasped the briefcase handle, seeming unaware that she did so, and walked out the front door with her second son behind her. Dalmar admired Ani's smarts, as well as his oversized balls.

"You might be useful," Dalmar said, and he walked away.

CHAPTER NINETEEN

Cullen was the first person in line to get off the ship when the announcement came that passengers could disembark. He patted the right front pocket of his black khaki shorts to make sure the nylon cord was still securely coiled inside. He had chosen the shorts because they had extra pockets for whatever eventuality. His black pullover shirt might prove a bit warm for the day, but he thought it made him inconspicuous and unremarkable. His socks and sneakers were also black. Focused on his mission, Cullen moved down the boarding ramp with the other passengers.

Jen wasn't far behind, maybe about three minutes. Her yellow bikini was visible through a white see-through beach top, and she loved the sexy feel of her newest designer jeans shorts. As she moved along in line, she reached to pull her thick long ponytail through the back of her Florida Gator baseball cap. Jen hoped to attend the University of Florida after high school graduation, and she liked to show her

allegiance to her future school. The cheap pair of sunglasses

she'd picked up at Target were too big for her face, but the

super dark lenses suited her requirements. The straw bag

dangling from her shoulder contained a towel, suntan lotion,

a book, the necklace she had stolen the night before, and, of

course, her cell phone. She was under explicit orders to text

her mother every half hour, no challenge for nimble teenage

texting fingers.

As Jen touched the firm, wharf pavement, quite a

change from the undulating deck motion, an amazing sense

of freedom came over her. She was really being trusted to be

on her own. She fingered the necklace in her bag and giggled

to herself that she had been so bold and so lucky to not have

been caught. Then her thoughts quickly turned to guilt as

she realized the ramifications of what she'd done. Still,

pausing for a moment to contemplate, she shrugged then

took out the necklace and put it around her neck, patting it with great satisfaction as she imagined sunlight flashing off the silver accenting her pretty neck.

Jen clipped along at a fair pace. A short walk down the pier landed her at the beach gate. She followed the path to the left and she could see that another short walk would take her to good vantage points. On the right was the shopping mall, which Jen figured she would explore later. First she would secure herself a spot on the beach and establish her position. She hadn't gotten a hundred yards before she heard her cell phone pinged.

Where the heck r-u? Just kiddin. Have a good time!

Walking down the beach, Jen texted back to her mom

—

Fell off dock. Am being rushed to hospital! W/let you know how the food is.

****

Cullen made his way through the crowded mall. He breathed steadily, evenly. He had trained himself over the years not to show any signs of nervousness. That kind of thing got you noticed and he wanted to appear to be, in every way, a typical American tourist. He stopped in a jewelry shop and looked at some rings, taking time to have the salesperson pull out several for him to inspect more closely. Deciding on one, he told the clerk he would be back later to purchase it. The clerk, assuming this tourist would not be back, stepped up his selling technique, but Cullen was much more interested in making sure the clerk remembered him than he was in buying. He was also interested in making sure the in-store cameras videotaped him, full face. If he came back, there would be a record of where he'd been and what he'd done, just in case.

With each stop along his route, anticipating what was to come, Cullen felt his heart beat harder. Heart and mind worked as one to focus his energy on his coming kill. This was part of the addictive lure of this all-consuming drug of his.

Seeing a clothing store window festooned with screaming-loud Hawaiian print shirts, he entered and picked out one he could come back for if he needed to. *Always have several back-up plans,* he thought; *the sign of a good serial killer.* In Cullen's mind, such care marked a serial killer who had never been caught, or even suspected. Again, he felt a twinge in his loins and then the accelerated beating of his heart. *God, he was good.* His killing wasn't about sex, oh no, but it still stirred his urges. His body never let him down, becoming an orgasmic symphony, ebbing and flowing before, during, and after the kill. He didn't dwell on the sexual nature of his response; that was too much like other, inept, serial killers. No, he preferred to see the rush like a runner's high.

The instant of the kill pumped adrenaline and gallons of other stimulants through his body, but everything leading up to it gave him a series of thrills, and he was jolted by a powerful high right afterwards. That euphoric rush would sometimes last for days, even weeks, and when it began to dissipate, his razor-sharp memories could summon the feeling back, no sweat. In his photographic memory he filed each killing by number to be recalled instantly and at will.

Cullen remembered hearing how baseball great Reggie Jackson said he could recall each and every one of his five hundred and sixty-three life-time home runs. Reggie could name the ballpark, name the pitcher, quote the count, and recall the type of pitch he had slugged for the homer. Cullen, like Reggie, remembered the place, his weapon, the time of day. He actually smelled whatever had been in the air, and most of all could see, with tremendous clarity, the victim's death grimace and the gasp of his final breath, moist and hot. Surely, if Mr. October remembered five-hundred and sixty-three homers, Cullen could remember his smaller but so much more significant number. The number fifty pulsated in his brain like a neon flasher.

Cullen increasingly focused and lost in his emotions and objectives overlooked something. He had picked up a tail.

CHAPTER TWENTY

Dalmar believed his plot was so bold that it would be talked about for all time as the greatest of oceanic hijackings. Someday, someone would have to make a movie of it. Through Korfa Osman's connections, they had acquired all their weapons, which included five AK-47 assault rifles, numerous handguns, knives, various other implements of destruction, and even a grenade launcher. They also received white ship-style uniforms for five pirates and blue coveralls, complete with company logos and name tags, for the rest. Ani, the newest member of the team, would have to wing it, but he was to stay in one of the shuttle ships anyway, so he would wear what he normally did to pilot his boat.

The two shuttle ships had long rows of benches for passengers, with ample storage underneath where the pirates could conceal their weapons. It was critical that everything appear normal, routine, and unremarkable. The liner's staff would begin shuttling passengers around nine a.m. and would continue the process of putting them off on OAR Cay until eleven a.m. Once the bulk of the passengers got off the ship, Dalmar's mission would begin in earnest.

While Dalmar dropped the final details of his plan into his brain's data slots, Captain Gunnar called down to cabin 9500 to find out how things were going. Jo informed him that Robby's condition was not much improved, and that Jen had gone into town on her own. Gunnar sent the doctor to Jo's cabin.

The doctor asked a few questions and palpated Robby's abdomen. The tightness in the boy's belly started the medic thinking that maybe this wasn't food poisoning, after all. Dr. Trainon believed it was rare for an eight year-old to have appendicitis, but that's what this seemed like. Trainon wasn't the best at remembering stuff like that anymore, nor was he very good at diagnosing medical

conditions. In fact, Dr. Trainon wasn't much of a doctor.

He'd finished his degrees and practiced for a while but was

caught illegally selling prescription drugs in his native

Switzerland. His medical career was derailed. What was to

have been a couple of years' suspension, turned into almost

three decades. By the time he'd gotten back into medicine,

he had forgotten most of what he knew — his own drug

dependence erased the rest. Trainon had a friend who

forged his records enough to get him a job with the cruise

company; he was lucky that most of his duties involved

doling out drugs for dysentery and cleaning up small

scrapes and infections. Anyone seriously injured was flown

to a hospital by helicopter. No worries that Trainon would

ever have to deal with reality. Now he had to decide

whether or not to panic and send Robby to the hospital on

St. Thomas. Trainon figured a bad diagnosis would cost the

company helicopter or ambulance fees and might possibly cost him his job. If the kid really did have appendicitis, Trainon would be vindicated. If the kid died, Trainon was screwed. He decided to stand pat for now and continue to monitor the boys' temperature and condition. If the fever continued to rise or there was acute abdominal pain, he would get Robby off the ship and out of his hair. If the fever subsided, Trainon would be in the clear. The thermometer currently read 99.5, not high enough for alarm or even much concern.

Jo tried to read while Robby slept, but in ten minutes she felt fidgety so she stretched out on the balcony chaise for about fifteen minutes. Restless again, she called room service and ordered brunch, hoping food and a movie might distract her. She wondered why the Captain had not sent Penny today so Jo could take a short break; but it occurred to her that if not for the Captain taking a liking to her, they would not have gotten this much attention. A thought dangled in

her troubled mind as she dozed off; *did I do the right thing*

letting Jen get off the ship alone on a strange tropical island?

CHAPTER TWENTY-ONE

Elaine Nickels had no doubt her husband was a sick person. She knew he was the sanest and nicest mentally ill person she'd ever been around and she loved him. His banking career had set them up nicely in retirement and that money funded these lavish vacations she so loved. She enjoyed the gambling and the drinking. She loved that she could gamble and drink without worrying about money. She was never concerned for her own safety with her husband, but she did worry that someday his side business could, yes, *would* get out of control. She was never sure who fell victim to his dark side, and she didn't want to know. Cullen always seemed in control. She thought the way he took care of his business was quite ingenious, and it worked out well for them both. She got to go on her trips and he indulged in the horrible things he needed. Looking the other way was morally wrong, but that transgression came with

immeasurable benefits.

She'd known for years. The first time she thought

something was amiss was nearly twenty years ago on a trip

to the Bahamas. He left early in the morning and when he

returned that evening he was wearing a different shirt and

hat. She noticed a blood stain on his sock and small cuts on

his hand. She pretended she didn't see, and so began

building a comfort zone for him; let him believe she knew

nothing. The more oblivious she seemed, the more

comfortable he'd gotten with leaving little things out in the

open. Stolen steak knives, odd belts and shoelaces, laundry

lines missing in the bathrooms — oh, she noticed, but he

never believed she could focus on details through her

alcoholic haze. After the early sock incident, the blood stain,

he stopped wearing socks. She silently applauded how he

learned from mistakes and honed his craft. Her future was

secure if his was. Now, when she allowed her conscience to get her attention, she debated which one of them was actually sicker.

Elaine often wondered and feared what would happen if his side business were discovered. She fretted briefly about how that would affect her life, but it had been going on so long that she found it easier to stifle her concerns and head for the casino or the spa. Sometimes she was downright amazed that he had not been discovered. A deep shiver crawled up her spine each time she saw him sitting at a bar table with an umbrella cocktail in front of him. She knew that meant he had completed a "business transaction." The shiver always gave way quickly to a robust sigh. Another success for her beloved and no sign that anyone knew what he had done. Each time, Elaine smiled and placed a lipsticky kiss on his bald spot. Once again, nothing would change in her world.

As soon as Cullen had walked out the door on this morning, Elaine was up and into the shower. Within a few minutes she dressed and hurried out the door. She had a chilling compulsion to see her husband in action, but had no courage to really pursue him. She walked across the ship down the flights of stairs towards deck five where passengers were disembarking.

"Hello," she said with a fake smile glued to her mouth as she passed people. "Good morning." *Get the fuck out of my way.* She couldn't lose sight of her man.

She went down each level of stairs methodically, making sure she could still see Cullen and he could not see her. It probably looked as though her head were on a swivel as it swung back and forth, sort of like a big cat stalking game on an African plain. She passed decks eight and seven, then deck six where she turned and stopped for a moment. Elaine, as always, contemplated following her husband all the way and wondered if it would change things if she witnessed his grisliness. She stood for several long minutes, lost in her thoughts. Cullen, slightly below her and ahead, shifted his glance in her direction and she ducked behind a tall man and counted ten before she peaked out again. Her husband had not seen her this time, either. She watched him walk off the gangplank then pivoted on one foot and headed for the casino.

CHAPTER TWENTY-TWO

Jen watched Mr. Nickels pass right by her on her way to the gangplank as they disembarked with the crowd. For the first time since she'd met him, he wasn't smiling or laughing. *Odd that he didn't even say hello as he passed. He looked almost like he was in a trance.* Maybe he didn't recognize her in the hat and glasses, but that shouldn't have changed the way he acted towards other people. He was way quiet and kept his eyes straight ahead. No jokes, no social small talk, no offers of assistance. Seeing him again after a text to her mother, Jen decided to change her plans slightly and observe him for a while before she continued on to the beach. For some reason, she found herself captivated by this man. She felt compelled to watch him and felt deeply drawn to him. The feelings were dark, uncomfortable, but undeniable, like when she had taken the necklace. She knew she could be headed for trouble, but she couldn't care.

She watched him walk purposefully past a few shops.

Cullen's first stop was the open mall where he went into a

jewelry shop and stayed for quite a while. Mrs. Nickels

didn't seem to wear jewelry, so Jen wondered if he was

having some kind of affair. *A bracelet for a girlfriend?* The teen

giggled, trying hard not to picture this old guy with a hot

date. She sat down on a wrought iron bench next to a faded

wooden Indian and watched Mr. Nickels through the shop

window. After a few minutes, Jen pulled out her book,

Population One, and began to read, quickly sinking into the

rich plot. The hero, Rana, was a girl about the same age as

Jen and was on her own in a strange place, too. Jen read a

few pages, looking up at each change of paragraph. When

Mr. Nickels came out the jewelry store door, he had no

package or parcel in hand. He didn't notice Jen sitting there

reading. As he turned to the right and started to walk, Jen

got up and followed. She saw him enter a clothing shop and

darted in after him, ducking behind a tall crowded rack of

muumuu's and lounge dresses. She watched him go through

a display of shirts and move one out of its order to place it in

the back of the rack. Then he did the same with a hat,

moving it from where it was to a different spot. Feeling a

creepy prickling of her skin, she left the store before him. *No

sense getting caught, right?* She actually began to think she

was having fun now, pretending to be Nancy Drew, and she

so liked her move of leaving the store first. How cool to

follow someone from in front of them. Cullen still hadn't

noticed her; she turned her face away from him and ordered

an ice cream from a vending cart while her quarry exited the

store.

Next, Cullen went into a small sundry store and

purchased a magazine and a bag of what looked to be

smoked almonds. He strode toward the busy intersection

across from the mall. They were becoming engulfed by a

growing crowd of tourists so keeping out of his line of sight was still not difficult. When he got across the street, Jen watched him tuck the magazine under his left armpit and then open his bag of almonds. She didn't feel much satisfaction from his actions, maybe her instincts were wrong and Mr. Nickels would prove to be a crashing bore.

The crowd thinned out near him, making it difficult to keep up the tail, and Jen considered quitting the game in favor of sun and surf. At this point, if he caught her it would be difficult to explain why she was in his path so far from attractions that appealed to teens. As she formed that thought, he went into the Al Coheri Liquor Mall and she figured the jig was just about up. No way could she go into a liquor store without drawing suspicion. Then she saw the sign that said, *Also Serving Pizza*, and knew she had the potential for a decent alibi if he spotted her. This was still fun.

Cullen looked around the store for a short time as Jen watched him from a corner. She carefully stayed as far from him as she could, so she lost him as he went around corners in the fair-sized liquor store. For no reason, she took the phone out of her bag and pretended to be in a conversation. And again for no reason, she clicked over to the photo setting and took photos of the store and of Mr. Nickels as he left.

****

A knock on the cabin door wakened Jo from a deep slumber. Oddly, it had been a satisfying sleep, probably the best rest she'd had since the trip began. When she opened the door, Drago Stevinski the security chief from Bulgaria stood in a kind of attention stance, his officer's cap under one arm. He nodded.

"Is everything going well here?" he asked.

"Yes. I mean he's still not feeling all that good," she nodded towards Robby, "but we're doing ok."

"That is good," he said. "Madam, I am here to talk with you about another matter that has come up and is in need of your immediate attention."

Jo's mind raced and her heart fluttered as she realized she had not heard from Jen in quite a while. She let her baby out on her own, and Jen was in trouble!

"What is it? Has something happened to Jen at the beach?"

Drago looked at her, puzzled for a moment.

"No madam, nothing has happened to your daughter in town that I know of, and I am sorry to startle you." He opened up a manila folder, removed a picture, and handed it to her. "This is your daughter, am I correct?" Without waiting for her answer, he continued, "Last night, our security cameras taped her walking away with the necklace she is wearing in this picture."

"This can't be Jen. She was with me last night." Jo realized it was obvious she was trying to protect her daughter until she could hear Jen's side of the story. In her career as a journalist, Jo had criticized so many parents doing the same, without thinking, when a child was in trouble. *I'm like them*, she thought, *when confronted; I immediately created an alibi to help my child.* Jo realized there would be a whole lot more explaining to do later if the facts proved her wrong. The necklace was not familiar to her, and she was trained to gather facts, not leap to conclusions. She stopped talking, deciding to listen.

"I have discussed this matter with Captain Gunnar, and he assumes," Drago cleared his throat, frowned, and continued, "that the young lady accidentally walked off with the necklace, forgetting to pay. He tells me that if you produce the necklace and bring it back to the store this evening, the mistake will be overlooked. Will that be satisfactory?" Drago's eyes were accusing. It was clear he and the captain didn't agree with this way of handling the situation, but Drago clamped his jaw shut, locking eyes with Jo.

He stood accusing her daughter of being a criminal and, at the same time, passing judgment on what he thought was going on between her and Captain Gunnar. Much as she itched to slap his smug face, she chose restraint and acquiescence, at least until Jen returned and this could get squared away.

"I'm sure this is a simple misunderstanding. My daughter is off the ship right now, but I can assure you, if she has the necklace we will return it the moment she comes back."

Drago nodded and stepped away, but in a second, Jo called out to him, "Um, Mr. Drago — would you mind if I held onto that photograph?"

He came back and turned it over to her, the smug smirk crawling back across his face. "Not at all, madam. We have copies and we have the security camera video that the still shot was taken from."

Jo shut the door and stood with her back against its cool surface. Cheeks flaming, she studied the photograph for several moments. It was definitely Jennifer. What else did she not know about her daughter? *Was Jen hiding secrets? How is that possible?* Jo wondered if the marvelous open relationship they seemed to have was a façade and Jennifer felt like all the other teenagers. *Was the child just skilled at hiding things?* Jo's heart grew heavy; worry seemed to crush even closer to her than it had for the past days. She thrust herself away from the door and pulled open the drawer where Jen's things were stored. Jo was determined to find the necklace and confront her daughter with it when she returned. *How could Jen do this?* The Captain was involved, as well. *Good God, what does he think of us after all his kindness and attention?* She became more and more embarrassed and anger mounted inside her. One phrase resonated in her head as she searched. *Vacation from hell.*

On cue, Robby sat up straight in the bed. "Mom, my stomach hurts; I'm gonna puke again."

CHAPTER TWENTY-THREE

What the hell am I doing? Jen had been playing

detective and following Mr. Nickels around for over an

hour. She'd wasted a chunk of beach time, all in all, and for

what? She wondered how much of her mother she had in

her and how many times Jo probably did the same thing

during her journalism career. Still, Jen watched Mr. Nickels

leave the liquor store, make a right up a hill, and go into a

dumpy looking bar, Razzy's, the sign said. She wondered

why anyone on vacation in the tropics would choose such a

filthy looking place. Maybe he was a government official, a

spy even, going to secure some kind of top secret

information.

She resolved that the same sun warmed her hanging

out here as would shine on her if she were at the beach, so

she picked a shade tree in the open field facing the side of

the bar. Tossing her bag to the ground, she sat down with

her back to the tree trunk. She could see both the rickety

front door and the beaten up back door that was half door

and half some kind of flimsy make-shift screen. Behind the

place was an alley way overgrown with shade trees and

palms. The wall of greenery hid the shack from the town just

beyond and above it. If you were standing anywhere in the

town above the bar you wouldn't see it at all. Once again,

Jen opened her book and began to read, but remembered it

was about time to text her mom. She laid the book down in

the seared grass and thumbed a message,

All is fine. Relaxing under a big palm. How's bro?

****

Jo's phone beeped as the thermometer in Robby's

mouth sounded. His temperature had reached 100.8 and he

wasn't looking better. She put the thermometer down and

read her daughter's latest message. Jo came close to ordering

the kid's ass back to the ship, but decided that would give

her daughter too much time to concoct a story. Jen could finish her day on her own, and Jo would save the confrontation for when she could look her daughter directly in the eye. Her temperature felt hotter than Robby's when she pounded out her response.

Temp still rising. Enjoy your time.

Jen read the screen, tucked the phone into her pocket, and went back to the teen fantasy.

In the bar, Cullen couldn't believe his good fortune. He spotted not one, but two candidates as soon as he walked into Razzy's. As dumps went, this place really took the cake. The ancient wood floor had rotted long ago. Splinters curled in semi-circles around the edges. Faded posters plugging different brands of beer, some that no longer existed, hung everywhere on the walls. The duct tape that once held the shredded bar stools together was grimy and stringy, having become the actual seat cushion in some cases, and the rest were deteriorated slabs of ass-rotted foam. A few bottles of

half-empty Jack Daniels and some other bottles of almost

empty rum languished behind the bar, but cheap beer was

clearly the drink of choice. Buy one, and nurse it for hours.

An easy place to hang out. Cullen figured the asses planted

on those perches these days were long-time Razzy regulars.

No doubt these guys never saw anyone other than

neighborhood drunks, and they were probably startled to

see him walk in, a middle-aged, milky white, very American

tourist.

Cullen grabbed a corner stool; the most damaged of

them all, and immediately felt a poke to his butt from what

felt like a nail. Trying not to flinch, he threw his magazine

down on the bar. An old black woman, probably in her

middle fifties but looking much older and worn out, carried

a box out of the back room. She also carried about eighty

pounds of body fat on her and had dark skin that was

wrinkled like it had been left out in the sun too long. The once colorful bandana on her head had long ago faded and her once white tank top was grungy and crumpled. Her flabby arms bounced and jiggled as she walked. She burst out laughing when she saw Cullen sitting at the bar.

"Well, *you* must be lost. I haven't seen your skin color in here since St. Thomas rose from the ocean."

When she said *rose from the ocean,* her voice rose like it came from a preacher delivering a sermon.

Cullen chuckled, too. "Today's your lucky day. Whitey has arrived, and he needs a drink. How's about one of them local island beers? Got anything kind of light? I intend on drinking quite a few!"

"Why you want to be drinkin' dis early in the morning, Mr. Whitey? And we ain't had nuthin' light in here…"

"Wait, let me guess," Cullen interrupted her. "Since *St. Thomas rose from the ocean.*"

"That's right," she cackled. "I like you, Whitey. What ship you with? And you got anything you like to go by other than *Whitey* — lest I keep calling you that?"

Cullen actually preferred Whitey right now.

"Whitey's fine, I'm on the *U.S. Pretentious* — -you know the one with all the uptight Americans I couldn't wait to get away from. I like you, as well. So what happened to those two?" Cullen pointed to two men sleeping or passed out on the floor in a corner.

"Oh, those two bums they had a bet last night — who could drink the most and then last the longest without going home. Dey each is more stupid than the other, but dey both don't have no give-up in 'em. By the way, you can call me 'Esmerelda,' if you like." She popped the top of a beer and slid it across to Cullen. He took a quick swig.

"Not bad, Esmerelda. So what was the prize?"

She looked at him, her eyebrows drown together and her lips pursed. "Huh?"

"What does the winner get when the other one finally goes home?" he clarified.

"Oh, I get you," she said. "*I* de prize!" She thumped her chest, puffed out her bulging breasts, and put her hands on ample hips.

"You don't think I give dis shit away for nuthin', do ya?"

They both laughed and Esmerelda retreated into the back room, shaking her butt and swaying her hips. One of the men woke up and stumbled into the restroom. Cullen decided he would wait for the first to leave and take the second as his victim. It crossed his mind to do them both if they left together. When the man came out of the bathroom, he wobbled and grabbed his head, moaning. He bent over for a moment, then stood upright and made it out the door.

The bright sunlight nearly knocked him back into the

barroom and Cullen half rose, thinking he might be missing

an easy mark. Thinking better of it, he opened his magazine

and slowed his breathing.

Halfway through Cullen's third beer and part way

through his magazine, he watched the second man pull

himself up off the floor and head for the restroom. Cullen

placed more than enough money on the bar and followed his

potential prey into the bathroom so as to size him up. The

killer stood at the sink squinting into the cloudy, broken

mirror, summing up the slob who had preceded him into the

john. The fellow's grey hair stood straight up with a few

dark and greasy wisps plastered around the ears. A

significant scar under the right eye looked like it might have

gotten there in some kind of fight. The drunk's filthy shorts

bagged at his hips, and he hadn't bothered to tuck in his

faded island shirt. The man took a long piss, oblivious to Cullen studying him in the mirror, and then he zipped up and stumbled over to contemplate his condition in the mirror. Cullen pretended to wipe his hands, slowly and carefully.

"Shit," the victim said, and he splashed water on his leathery black face. He honked his nose into a paper towel before wiping his face with it. Cullen felt his gorge rise. The fellow was a pig. The pig stared directly into the mirror at his own bloodshot eyes; his stupid expression gave way to a joyful grin. "I won!" he hooted, "I fucking won!"

****

Jen had fallen asleep under her tree. She woke up to the vibrations of her phone. Glancing down, she saw a text from her father.

How's the trip going? Miss you guys. Hug Robby for me. Love you.

While she started to type her response, a wispy haired man left from the back door of the bar and she watched Mr. Nickels leave from the front and circle towards the back. Odd.

Miss you too. She tapped. *Robby came down with something. Met the Captain. Hangin in St. Thomas right now, chillin.*

She dispatched the message and looked up to see Cullen Nickels follow the wobbling man behind the bar. Nickels glanced behind his left shoulder and then pulled something from his right pants pocket. Interested, Jen slipped behind the tree for cover. Before she could puzzle out his actions, Cullen had the clothes line from his pocket around the man's neck, and he pulled it tight with such force that the man's feet came off the ground. Jen opened her mouth to scream. No sound came out.

While the man flailed, grappling and clawing behind his head to thwart his attacker, Jen felt helpless. She couldn't physically intervene. Screaming would be disastrous. So, she did what any teenager with a phone in her hand would do. She snapped a picture. Then she took another, and another. By this time, Cullen stood over his victim who was still gasping for air. Cullen bent down, placing one arm securely under the man's chin and a second on the guy's forehead. Nickels torqued his body with enough force to turn the already spasming, rigid body to jelly. The man stopped moving.

Jen snapped again, trembling and feeling a terrible need to pee. She had, at some point, thrown herself to the ground and now lay on her belly. Her labored breathing caused physical discomfort. Adrenaline flooded through her and she leaped up and sprinted, with no thought or plan, toward the front door of the bar.

Cullen, lost in rapture, admired his work for a moment. The big five-oh. He absorbed the scene; the corpse, the glazed eyes, feint but growing ligature marks. He breathed in the air around the body as one might take in the bouquet of a fine shiraz. He unraveled the cord partially embedded in his victim's neck, stood up, and began to stroll away. Fifty yards down the hill; his mellow mood was interrupted by the clanging of garbage cans back near the bar.

Jen had crashed into the metal cans as she lunged for the front door of Razzy's. She picked herself up off the ground and slammed the door against the wall as she careened through the opening and fell into the dark tavern.

"Hep...Man...Hep...Back..." Her words would not flow. She couldn't yell for help. Usually calm and controlled, she couldn't tolerate her own hysteria. Esmerelda, hearing the commotion, rushed from the back room and stared at Jen.

"Two whitey's in one day? What is happ'nin' to dis island?" She grumbled to herself as she bent laboriously over, grabbed Jen's arm, and lifted the girl, not at all ungently.

"Say what you got to say, girl. What the problem?"

Still gasping and wheezing, Jen couldn't form the words. She reached for her phone. It wasn't in her pocket.

****

Cullen strode down the hill at a faster pace than he normally would have. Worried about the sound from above, he thought it possible he had been seen, but he wasn't sure. He had to commit, going back could mean getting caught. Making his choice, he quickened his step so he could get back to the mall and implement his now-needed backup plan. He looked back over his shoulder toward the bar and saw Jen burst out the front door and trip over garbage cans then she bent and scrambled in the dust. Out of his earshot, Cullen's new friend Esmerelda followed the girl out and watched as Jen crawled on hands and knees looking for her phone. Jen, somewhat recovering her voice, croaked out, "Call an ambulance. There's a dead guy in your back alley!"

Esmerelda almost cackled, but apparently the look on the girl's face showed her that she was serious.

"What you say, girl?" Esmerelda turned and dashed through the bar and out the back door.

Jen located her phone, sobbing out relief, and a second later, Esmerelda's scream tore the air.

Cullen heard it and felt ill. He wasn't sure changing his clothes would get him out of this one. He wasn't sure anything could get him out of this one. Cullen forced himself into a sprint.

CHAPTER TWENTY-FOUR

Jen wasn't waiting for Esmerelda to come back. She started down the hill, back toward the ship. Phone in hand, she stabbed out a message to her mother while she ran and skidded and scrubbed tears from her face.

Coming back. Saw something horrible. Need help! Scared!!!

Jo heard her phone beep and figured it was just Jen's check-in. Robby's temperature had increased to 101.3 and was still rising. She called for the ships' doctor and then she called for room service while she waited. She was too busy to worry about a message.

****

At the mall, minutes ahead of Jen, Cullen slipped into the clothing store and grabbed the items he had pre-placed. He paid with cash and ducked into a restroom right outside the shop. He changed clothes, found the cord he had wrapped around his victim's neck, dropped it into a toilet, and flushed. Not wasting another second, he got back to the ship and boarded, knowing Jen had seen something. *But what?* How long had she been up there? He hoped she had only seen a man in a black shirt, and when she described what she saw, it would be different from the way he looked when he re-boarded. Now he needed as many people as possible to see him in his touristy Hawaiian style clothes. His thoughts nagged him. *What the hell was Jen doing outside that bar?*

****

Jogging now, winded, Jen texted her mom,

Call Captain Gunnar. Just witnessed something horrible. Don't know what to do. Be back soon.

Again, Jo ignored her beeping phone. She was in no mood to start the inevitable battle with her daughter. For at least the tenth time, she gently laid the back of her cool hand against Robby's fiery brow and prayed the doctor would knock on the door.

On the hill, Jen felt calmer, but still frightened, wondering why her mother did not respond. She tried again,

Mom. I think I just saw someone murdered! Where r u?

****

Esmerelda looked at the body, not knowing whether to laugh or cry. She didn't waste time, but grabbed an arm and began to drag the fresh corpse into her bar.

"You sorry ass dumb shit gone and got you self killt," she cajoled. "What I supposed to do now? Who do dis to you?"

She pulled the body inside, lifted it, and pushed with her considerable strength until it thunked down into a rusted flattop freezer in the back room. Maybe she should have just left the bastard in the bar and hoped everyone thought her husband had finally drunk himself to death.

Except that his head was almost twisted clear off and there was a bright, straight, red mark on his throat where he had obviously been strangled.

"You so stupid they had to kill you twice!" she complained, glaring at her husband whom she had just shoved into a freezer. "I don't need this kind of trouble."

She slammed the freezer and padlocked it.

****

Jo got her turkey sandwich from room service and wondered how they could fulfill their duties faster than a doctor did. She had her mouth full of the last bite of sandwich when Dr. Trainon knocked on the door. All the while he had been walking to the room, the doctor silently implored whoever might care about his concerns that this boy's problem would vanish into thin air. The man did not want to go inside that cabin. He did not want to do any real doctoring. He was a fraud, and he knew it. He paused at the door for a long, long time before he knocked.

"Sorry it took me so long," he lied. "I was attending to a very sick older gentlemen. I have put together a few prescriptions for Robby. First, I would like him to take this pill for pain, and then this antibiotic."

He placed the bottles on the nightstand and walked into the bathroom, where he got a glass of water for Robby. He hoped to God that a little pain medication and some antibiotics would buy enough time to turn this into someone else's problem. He was pretty sure they were dealing with an appendicitis attack. If he could get the symptoms to subside, would he get himself out of this situation?

"Why does he need pain medication for food poisoning? Or antibiotic's for heaven sake," Jo demanded. "I mean, what about something for nausea?"

Dr. Trainon felt sticky droplets of sweat trickle from his armpit down his side, dampening his cotton uniform shirt. He grasped for an answer in his foggy brain. He had nothing. He found himself seeking divine intervention, but knew it was no use for someone as belief-less as himself.

Then divine intervention seemed to descend upon him. Jo's cell phone beeped insistently. The doc pointed to the phone, stammered something in an attempt to forestall the inevitable. Jo grabbed the phone to silence it, but something caught her eye and she read all three of Jen's messages.

Coming back now. Just saw something horrible. Need help. Scared!!!

Call Captain Gunnar. Just witnessed something horrible. Don't know what to do. Be back soon.

Mom. I think I just saw someone murdered! Where r u?

Jo clamped her hand over her mouth feeling as though *she* might vomit this time. "Listen," she babbled,

"Stay a moment with Robby, will you? I have to see to something!" She tore out of the room without another glance at the doctor who blotted beads of perspiration off his forehead for a second before he gave Robby the pills.

****

People who lived in the few blocks around Razzy's knew that Esmerelda's first husband, the namesake of the bar she now owned, had beaten her on a daily basis. Still, they liked Razzy and most had never swallowed the story that he'd fallen down in a drunken stupor and had broken his neck. But for the most part they looked the other way. It wasn't their business, if they thought about it, really. It had taken some years, but Esmerelda had regained their confidence and affection. As long as the beer was cheap and almost cold, all could be overlooked. Then, she married the dumb stiff who was now hardening in her freezer, and it started to happen again. Ok, he had beaten her, but she hadn't killed this one. This is where Cullen got a huge stroke of good fortune. To Esmerelda, it didn't seem plausible that she wouldn't be accused of murder this time. She knew the local police didn't have much in the way of science to prove her innocence and she knew it was more than likely she'd be guilty until proven otherwise. Better to chop the bastard up and get rid of him, piece by piece.

****

Jo sprinted down to the deck two gangplank two seconds after Cullen Nickels had walked past and headed straight up to customer relations. There he started a quick conversation with Doratai, a young Croatian girl working behind the counter. About the same time, Jen came sprinting up the gangway and was stopped by security.

"Ma'am, we need to see your shipboard identification in order for you to pass," the guard advised. Jen clearly saw in her mind; the scrub grass by the shade tree, where her

beach bag containing all of her identification was left.

"No, you don't understand," she shrieked. "I need to

get back on the ship. Please call the captain. He knows who I

am. I've got to get back on. I need my mom!"

The security guard stood between her and the

entrance. Jen, at her wits end, had no clue how to make him

understand. She grabbed his shirt sleeve, and got in his face

and then saw her mother round the corner at breakneck

speed.

"Jen!" Jo shouted. "What on earth is wrong? What's

going on?"

"Mama," Jen sobbed, reaching frantically for her

mother. "Oh my God oh God I'm so scared."

The security agent and his backup stood firm, a wall

between mother and daughter. Drago Stevinski showed up,

looking less than pleased at the commotion. "What is the

problem here?" he demanded, looming large and looking formidable.

Jen yelled at him, waving her arms, "I've got to get aboard! I don't have my ID with me — I lost it somewhere. Mom! Help me, Mom!"

Jo yelled, "Get your hands off my daughter!" and she moved forward, looking wild and desperate.

Drago stepped in front and took control. He'd had enough of these people. He couldn't let them jeopardize what would be happening tomorrow.

"Young lady, you are to calm down. Other passengers don't need this dramatic foolishness." He motioned the other security people to let her pass, then he grabbed her arm and walked her to Jo.

"Madam, I am turning her over to you for the time being." He beckoned to two of his officers. "These two men will escort you to your cabin, from which you are not to leave again under any circumstances. I will be by later to

sort out this mess. I can assure you, madam," he lectured,

"that I have seen every con there is, and none of what's gone

on with your family is new to me!" He turned to the two

officers and spoke again, "Take them to their cabin. Stand

outside it until further notice."

Now," he said to no one in particular, "get me

Captain Gunnar. Immediately!"

CHAPTER TWENTY-FIVE

Dalmar sat on the back porch of the house that he had claimed for his own over the past few days. He watched his men and his women kicking a soccer ball around, wanting to join them, but they were all well beneath his talent level. As much as he needed to dominate them, he knew that injuring them with his bruising style would not be good for tomorrow. He felt a smug sort of maturity having decided not to injure his own people.

Still watching, Dalmar thought about various scenarios that could occur and about various means of escape he might employ if necessary. He visualized each of his men and women and thought about when each would become expendable. Even Nadif, who was closest to him and had been with him for a long time — Dalmar could envision himself returning home without him, too.

He thought back to earlier times when things did not go according to plan. Once he'd hijacked a small yacht that was cruising through the Arabian Sea on a round-the-world trip. Usually, occupants of yachts had someone back home with lots of money who would be willing to pay for their safe return. The four people aboard this particular yacht were retired missionaries headed to hand out bibles in ports around the world. They had no money or valuables onboard and even the ship wasn't worth taking. Dalmar was minutes away from letting them go when one of the captives slammed a baseball bat into one of Dalmar's men, sending the pirate flying overboard. Another of Dalmar's team opened fire with a machine gun and blew the hero into the ocean. When another missionary came up to see what was going on, Dalmar's man shot him, as well. Dalmar removed the weapon from his henchman's hands and slowly walked down into the yacht, seeking the two crying wives. He gave them a short lecture.

"You're husbands were foolish men. Know this before you leave this world; I have never not gotten the ransom I wished from any ship I have pirated. You were less than two minutes from being freed, but your superhero husbands have literally killed all of you." He barely finished his sentence before he shot both of them.

"What a shame," he said, shaking his head. He turned to his man who had started the shooting and shot him in the leg, then ambled over to a storage area, picked up a gasoline can and dowsed the man with its contents. He did not listen to the man's pleas for mercy.

"I would not be who I am, nor command the respect that I do, if I were to let you live when you so foolishly ruined our chances of getting any ransom from this vessel." He figured it was better the rest of the men placed the blame on the itchy trigger finger of one fool man, than on him. He went back up top and told his men to get off the ship. As they all jumped across to their own vessel, he nodded at Nadif and said, "Torch it."

Another time, Dalmar and company had hijacked a tanker. The second in command of the captive ship found himself a nifty hiding spot in some hanging pipes, causing Dalmar to surmise that the man had escaped by jumping overboard — Dalmar and his crew had that effect on seconds. When Dalmar walked beneath him, the man could not resist being a hero; he pounced on Dalmar's head. The idiot dropped the knife he was holding as he fell, and Dalmar received a superficial shoulder wound. Dalmar was much stronger and far better trained in hand-to-hand. After toying with the fool for a while, Dalmar strung him up on the mast. This man and his foolhardy bravery would be a great example of what fury Dalmar was capable of. Dalmar's crew and the other captives would learn something and Dalmar would have some needed diversion

After stripping the man nude, Dalmar clipped the pinky toes off both the fellow's feet and dipped the open wounds into a bucket of salt water. The man passed out, but when he came to, Dalmar sliced him, with a filet knife, from his hips straight down the front of his legs all the way to his feet. Then he forced the man's remaining crew mates to throw bucket after bucket of salt water onto the gaping gashes. He left the man hang through the duration of the negotiations, which were completed surprisingly quickly.

CHAPTER TWENTY-SIX

Captain Gunnar and Chief Security Officer Drago Stevinski walked towards room 9500. It was six-thirty p.m. Half an hour earlier; the Captain had guided *the Treasure of the Seas* out of St. Thomas's port and toward the private island of OAR Cay. The ship was set at its cruising speed of 21.6 knots and was now in the capable hands of his crew. Trying again to get a handle on what had happened to him and his ship in the past few days, he had to admit it seemed to revolve around the Sampson family. He turned to Drago.

"So the girl says she saw another passenger kill somebody on St. Thomas?"

"That is correct, Captain," answered Drago.

"Was there a murder reported on the island today?"

"There was not, sir."

"What about a dead body? Did somebody have a heart attack, fall off a pier, or something — anything?"

Drago again shook his head in the negative without speaking.

"And the security cameras have the same girl on tape last night, stealing a necklace?"

"Yes, sir."

Gunnar stroked his chin and wrinkled his brow. "And you are absolutely, one-hundred percent sure it's the same girl — and that girl is Jennifer Sampson?"

"Yes, Captain," answered Drago, his color rising along with his temper. "My men and I have looked at the tape a hundred times. Clearly, it is the young lady from room 9500."

"Okay. I'm not questioning you and your staff's ability to do your jobs. I just want to be completely sure before I go in there."

They stopped a bit down the hall from the door to complete their discussion. Gunnar spoke. "One more thing,

Drago. If you had to explain this, what do you think happened?"

"Sir, I believe the young lady's mother tipped her off that she was caught on the security camera. To cover for herself, the girl concocted this ridiculous story about the murder, maybe hoping to gain her mother's and our sympathies. That would shift the focus from her theft."

"So you don't think the mother knew anything about the theft or the murder story?"

"No sir, I'm not yet willing to commit to the greater scenario you may be suggesting, unless I find out the boy is not as sick as he appears. If he's not sick, maybe there *is* a bigger grift going on."

"I doubt that. I've checked out the mother — she is a legitimate journalist with a good reputation. I'd wager she's no con."

"Sir, I know you checked out the mother," Drago said with a sly smile. "That is what worries me!"

The Captain returned the smile half-heartedly, "You don't worry about my motives, Drago, and I won't worry about yours." They proceeded to 9500 and Gunnar rapped on the door.

Jo, dressed in a t-shirt and shorts, opened the door and stepped aside for them to enter. Even though she wore no makeup and her hair was casually tossed, Captain Gunnar thought Jo was extremely satisfying on the eyes. Pulling his glance up to her face, he stopped himself from scanning her long darkly-tanned legs. Robby was sleeping. Jen had wrapped herself in a blanket and was huddled on the sofa-bed, staring blankly into space.

"How's your son?" the Captain asked.

"His temperature is over 102," she said. "This doesn't look like food poisoning to me."

"May I?" asked the Captain as he put his hand to Robby's forehead.

Jo stepped back, frowning.

"Wait a second," she said, sizing up the situation accurately, "You don't think he's really sick. You think we're *making this shit up?*"

"Nobody's jumping to any conclusions," answered the Captain, stealing himself for unpleasant outcomes. "We just need to find out more information."

Drago stepped forward now.

"Madam, may I ask your daughter a few questions about what she, er...*saw* today?"

"I don't know. Does she need a lawyer?" Jo snapped.

"Mom, it's okay. I'll answer his questions," Jen said.

"Thank you. Who did you see get murdered today, if I may ask?"

"I don't know — he was some drunken looking native guy."

"Where were you, exactly, when this murder occurred?"

"I don't know that either, somewhere in town."

"Where in town?"

"Behind some bar," Jen said, frustrated and feeling pressured.

"Honey, I thought you were at the beach today. What in the world were you doing at a bar?" This from Jo.

"That's just it; I wasn't actually *in* the bar. I was watching from the outside."

Jo's voice finally escalated as she abandoned all effort to remain impartial and objective, "What the hell were you doing watching a *bar* when you were supposed to be at the beach? This seriously keeps sounding worse."

"Please," Drago cut in, "allow me to ask the questions."

Jo took half a step, then regained her composure and bit her lip. Captain Gunnar stood in silence, not believing he had been on the verge of getting involved with this family. To his mind, the girl had now been caught stealing, lying, and fabricating a cover. Drago pursued.

"Once again," he said, clipping each word, "what was the name of the bar, and why were you there?" He smacked the back of one hand into the palm of the other to punctuate his questions.

"I don't remember the name of the bar. I *told* you." Jen shot back. Then she offered, "It was just up the hill, past the mall, and past some liquor store that serves pizza."

"Oh, dear God! You went to a liquor store and *then* to a bar!" her mother shouted, throwing her arms up. "I trusted you on your own and *this* is what you choose to do?"

Jen lowered her head. She trembled, partly out of anger at being accused of so many things at once, and partly in fear. What would happen to her if she couldn't square this? Jen decided to tell the whole truth. "I was following Mr. Nickels, alright? I watched him go into the liquor store and then into the bar." She took a breath and her eyes lighted up, "*Razzy's* was the name of the place! I remember it now."

"Who is Mr. Nickels?" asked the Captain.

Jo looked over her shoulder and responded. "He's the gentlemen two cabins over." Then, turning back to her daughter, she demanded, "What were you doing following Mr. Nickels?"

"I'm sorry, mom," Jen began to cry, unable to keep pace with this deteriorating fiasco. "For some reason, I followed Mr. Nickels off the ship and all the way to the bar. I know. It sounds stupid — but I did it, ok. I don't have a clue why. Th-then I saw him come out the back door and strangle some guy. He did it. I *saw it. I watched him.* I'm telling you, he's *crazy!*"

"Oh great," Jo threw her hands up again. "Now you're dumping some other passenger into your mess." She couldn't fathom where this convoluted story was coming from. What had gone wrong here? First the child is stealing, and then traipsing around to bars and liquor stores stalking some guy, then this incredible story.

Captain Gunnar stepped forward and sat on the sofa next to Jen. He put his left hand up, signaling the others to stop talking, and he laid his right hand on Jen's shoulder.

"Listen Jen, you're leveling pretty serious accusations against another passenger. Your mother and I want to believe you, of course. But to put it bluntly, right now you look like a teenage girl who got caught doing something you wouldn't normally do. Ok, you're scared, and I think you've concocted this story because you're afraid to tell the whole truth. I'm offering good advice: Don't make it worse. Right now, I'll ask your mom to calm down and promise not to get any angrier. It would be best if you just admit what you did. We'll have you pay for the necklace and all the rest of this goes away."

With nothing more he could do, the Captain stood up to leave, but addressed both Jo and Jen, "Please, talk this over. You have my word that if you pay for the necklace, I'll consider the matter closed."

Drago attempted to interrupt, but the Captain cut him off. "No, this ends it. Jo, I'll have Drago charge your credit card for the necklace." He took Jo by both shoulders, not ungently, and leaned close to her, speaking softly as if the two of them were alone in the room.

"Look, this is the best I can do. If you pursue it, I'll have to open an investigation. If I do that, it's entirely likely that U.S. law won't have jurisdiction and Jen will face another legal system. Do you understand that this may only get worse if we don't end it now?" Realizing that his words carried a double meaning, the Captain turned, opened the door, and motioned for Drago to go out ahead of him. He looked back one more time and nodded toward Robby.

"Do you need me to send the Doctor up to take another look at your son tonight?"

Mutely, Jo shook her head in a short negative.

"Tomorrow when Officer Drago is satisfied that the transaction is complete and you and your family feel safe, we'll relieve the guards and your cruise can go back to normal. Please feel free to order room service for tonight's dinner." He hated the look in Jo's eyes.

"Captain," Jen called out, right before he got out of the room. She bit her lower lip and spoke succinctly, "I *saw*

Mr. Nickels from room 9504 first strangle and then nearly twist the head off of somebody today."

The Captain lowered his head and shut the door.

CHAPTER TWENTY-SEVEN

At eleven p.m. sharp, Captain Gunnar left the bridge and retreated to his cabin. He took off his uniform and changed into the oversized t-shirt and gym shorts that he slept in. Then he tried to read for a few moments, but his eyes scanned and rescanned a single paragraph. His mind was stuck on Jo Sampson, exactly the type of woman that captivated him. She was in fact, so much like his first love, Sofia Caltimano, that they could have been incarnations of each other.

He'd never slept with Sofia and he regretted it to this day. His memories of her, he felt, would have been so much more vivid if they had consummated the relationship. He could still see her clearly, although his remembrances were turning grey and dismal like the old photograph he had just picked up from his nightstand. As he stared at Sophia's picture her face became Jo's, and he felt the same pain he had felt when he got the letter that Sophia had passed away. *When was that?* He was already a Captain, but years had passed. Wishing he could see her and hold her one more time, he placed her photograph back in the nightstand and wondered who he was becoming. Captain Gunnar Fredrickson did not act like this. He leaned back and tried to sort it all out.

Why did Jennifer steal the necklace? She hadn't seemed like a troubled teen, in fact, the family had seemed way above average. Why would she follow another passenger? And the boy, Gunnar conceded that the boy's forehead felt hot, but was he really sick? If this was a ruse or a con, what was the aim? To steal a necklace worth a few hundred dollars! It made no sense. Why would the girl accuse another passenger of such a hideous crime? Gunnar had read many stories of teenaged girls concocting elaborate lies out of jealousy or fear. Sometimes their victims were hurt, even sent away to prison for years before the girls

recanted. This girl didn't seem the type, but how could he

really know? No, none of it made sense. Deeply bothered, he

got up, left his quarters, and walked up the stairs to cabin

9504. He knocked on the door. Cullen Nickels opened the

door and looked shocked to see the Captain standing there

in a t-shirt and shorts. Though the hallway was warm,

Cullen's body felt chilled and an unusual shiver of fear ran

down his spine.

"Mr. Nickels, I'm Captain Gunnar. I'm extremely

sorry to bother you at this time, but I was wondering if I

might have a word with you?"

"Why, of course, Captain — the wife and I just got

back from the show. What's this all about?"

Elaine came out of the bathroom, and when she saw

the Captain her jaw dropped open in surprise. "Captain,

what an honor. To what do we owe this privilege?" She hoped to cover her concern.

"Well, Mrs. Nickels, I want to speak to your husband for a moment, if I could. Again, I'm sorry for the late hour and, more importantly, for the subject matter."

"Don't be silly. It's only eleven — that's practically mid-afternoon on a ship. But now you have me worried. I hope you aren't bringing bad news from home? Seeing you in civilian clothes, I fear the worst," Elaine said. She wasn't really concerned about family. They were childless and had no one at home to worry about, but she knew a visit from the captain at this hour could only be something terribly serious, and to Elaine, that meant her husband's dangerous activities. She felt in the pit of her stomach that she was about to see her weasel squirm.

"No, ma'am, it's nothing like that. Mr. Nickels, may we step outside for a moment?"

Elaine cut in, "Captain, I can assure you that whatever it is, I can handle it. Please don't delay any longer or my panic might get the best of me." She was playing with her husband now, like she'd seen him do so many times with others.

"What's on your mind?" Cullen said, coolly masking his building nervousness.

The Captain paused, choosing his words carefully. "The young lady two doors down from you believes she saw someone murdered today on St. Thomas."

Elaine gasped. "Who? Where?"

Gunnar turned to Cullen, "Well, I wondered if you could help me with that, sir." Cullen did not say a word. He showed no reaction other than a puzzled, questioning look on his face. "She says she was following you today, for some reason that neither she nor I could explain, and that you may have seen something, as well."

Cullen and Elaine both had reason to be shocked, so their reactions seemed appropriate to the ugly news Gunnar offered. All the years and all the kills had come down to this; it appeared the jig was up. Cullen could play it with outrage, or he could continue to feign concerned ignorance. Always preferring to play it close to the vest, he chose the latter.

"Well, I must say that would have been quite upsetting for the poor girl. What did she see?" he asked.

"Did you, by any chance, visit a bar today on St. Thomas?" Gunnar asked, choosing to avoid describing the incident.

"Heavens no, I most certainly did not. I rarely drink; visiting a bar wouldn't be my kind of thing."

"What did you do ashore then, sir?"

"Let me see," Cullen said, making a show of reaching into his memory, while he sought a way out of the corner he currently occupied. "I walked around the mall for a bit, window shopping more or less, stopped at a liquor store for

Elaine…" suddenly, the way out clicked in Cullen's mind.

"May I ask why this young lady followed me, Captain? I

saw her looking at me the other day, as well. Has she

developed some sort of obsession with me?"

"I guess that's what I'd like to find out," answered the

Captain.

Elaine thought her weasel had squirmed pretty well.

How quickly he'd latched onto the teenage girl obsession idea and

turned the child into the guilty party. Well played. But Elaine felt

white hot anger. He'd finally gone too far and suspicion

stalked him. Cullen was dangerously close to ruining her

life, her travels, her gambling; her fun.

Suddenly, Elaine laughed out loud, putting a hand on

Gunnar's arm, "Please. A pretty teenager obsessed with a

balding middle-aged man like Cullen?"

Gunnar couldn't remember ever having been this far out of his element. Where could he possibly take this mess tonight? If this guy was innocent, Gunnar was setting up a libel situation. And what if, by some weird chance, he was guilty? The whole thing was incredibly dangerous. "Look, I'm sorry I brought you into this," he told them. "If you don't mind, tomorrow I'll send my Chief of Security to your cabin for a statement from you. Just to get a timeline of your day. Forgive me for being so aggressive, but I must at least check the girl's story out. Better to do it sooner, rather than later."

"We understand," Cullen said as he put a loving arm around his wife. "I'll help you any way I can. By the way, *was* anyone killed today at a bar in St. Thomas?"

"No, sir," the Captain replied, "not that I know of." Cullen shut the door, drawing a slow, deep breath all the way from his toes.

Long, heavy moments ticked by in the Nickel's cabin.
Elaine continued to take off her clothes and her earrings,
getting ready for bed. Cullen broke the silence. "Well, there's
a first for you; a pretty teenage girl obsessed with me and
stalking me. How lucky for me."

Elaine stared right through him, pondering whether
to lash out or continue the pretense. She decided to stop
playing dumb. "What have you done? For years I've stood
by watching this obsession of yours. I've let it go
unchallenged. I never turned you in. All I've asked is that
my life not be destroyed. And now you get caught by a
teenage girl! How could you? How could you do this to
me?"

Cullen took in the whole diatribe, feeling himself
begin to sweat. His eyes grew very round and his hands
shook ever so slightly. *She knew? She couldn't know.* He took

such care. She'd never let on that she even had a clue. Now it was Cullen's turn at playing dumb.

He coughed a little and narrowed his eyes, "I have no clue what you're talking about, dear. I'm very confused. Obsession?"

"Don't play stupid with me, Cullen Nickels," she chided; her voice deadly quiet and even. "I've done enough of that for both of us all these years." She glared at him and continued, her jaw set and teeth clenched, "I will not have you screw up what I've got in my life. I will do whatever it takes to make it look like this kid has some kind of crush on you, if that's what will get you out of this. But be clear, when it's over and we get home, it is *over*! If you manage to get away with this one, you are officially *retired*. Do you understand? There will be no more of it. Can you do that for me, for *us*, Cullen? Can you turn it off?"

Abruptly, she clicked out the lights and got under the covers. Cullen stood in the dark, pondering whether he could stop his compulsion; quench his thirst for the thrills that drove his life. Finally, he too got into bed.

"Yes dear, I believe I can do that. I believe I can stop."

CHAPTER TWENTY-EIGHT

At five a.m. the weather shaped a perfect day; salt water licked and smacked the bottom of the two shuttle boats Dalmar and his crew were preparing outside of Chari Azar's former home. A single light attached to a pole along the dock helped them see what they were doing. In the distant blackness they heard someone whistling distinctively, drawing closer and closer.

"What the hell is that?" asked one of the men, as he drew a pistol.

Ani Azar peered into the blackness. "Please — draw down your weapon. It's our worker, Chill, hoping for a chance to earn money today. "Chill," he cried out, "is that you? There is no work today. Turn around and go home!"

Chill, in his own little world, grooved to the sounds pouring into his head through iPod ear buds. When he stepped into the light, he gaped at all the people aiming guns at him. Chill was a tall, lanky young man of about

twenty-two, with lean hard muscle, even though he

probably never exercised a day in his life. His skin was

slightly lighter than most St. Thomas natives. His long

dreadlocks, tied in a tight bundle, hung over the back of his

tank top. White pockets flagged out below the frayed edges

of his jean shorts, and Chill had to consciously squeeze his

toes together to keep from walking out of his ancient flip

flops. He'd been picking up odd jobs for years and Chari

Azar and his family had sort of taken him in, giving him

work when they could. He spent most of his time stoned,

but he realized early on that Chari would have no part of it,

so he was as straight as he could be when he showed up to

work the shuttle boats.

Now, Chill stood frozen at the site of uniformed men

and women loading equipment onto the boats while another

group waved weapons around. He slowly pulled his ear

buds out and looked at Ani. "Wow, my friend," he said, "Looks to me like you won't be in need of my services this morning." He moved carefully, backing up as he spoke.

"That's right," answered Ani. "Get a move on and get out of here."

"Not so fast," Dalmar cut in. "I think we can find a use for this man."

"Oh, hey boss, that's okay," replied Chill, eyeballing the firepower being loaded aboard. "I actually have to attend my cousins' bar-mitzvah today. So, um, I'll just be going." He heard the click of a gun cocking behind him, and reorganized his thinking. "Unless, of course, you really need some help today, then I'd be glad to chip in. No doubt." Chill's eyes met Ani's, and he whispered as he walked past his friend, "This is double time with hazard pay —am I correct my friend?"

Dalmar stood, one foot on the edge of a boat and the other on the dock, and addressed his crew. "People, listen to me. It is important that we communicate well today. Use your walkie-talkies at all times. You all know what your assignments are, so do your job first before helping someone else. Understand that this is a very big ship. I expect things will not go as easily as they do when we take a small yacht or a freighter. Be prepared to adapt. Be prepared to shed blood, although do not do it recklessly. Only use violence as a last resort. We are lucky this morning to be joined by a new member of our team. Meet Chill." He pointed in Chill's direction and the others nodded towards him.

"Maybe someday Chill can amuse us by explaining to us how he got his name. Right now, he and Ani will each drive one of the boats. I can assure you that when this is over, you will be very wealthy men. But if you make an attempt to sabotage our operation in any way — you will be very dead, un-wealthy men. Am I clear?"

Ani nodded. Chill said, "Wealthy and alive sound good to me. What do I do first?"

Dalmar ignored him and jumped aboard the first of the boats. "Let's go!" he ordered, and both boats began their short trek to OAR Cay.

****

Dalmar positioned himself next to Ani and studied him. He was almost positive that Ani would strike against him at some point. This young man did seem to possess keen insight and a certain coldness that worried Dalmar a little. He assumed that, given the death of the boy's father and the nature of this operation, Ani was coming up with a plan to escape. The trick was to anticipate Ani's moves and eliminate the boy right before anything happened.

"What is awaiting us when we get to the island?" asked Dalmar of Ani, while trying to speak above the whistling wind. "And please tell me something I don't already know."

Ani, too, shouted above the wind. "Two men stay on the island permanently. They will be there to greet us. One is young and very strong. The other is an older gentleman. After we drop some supplies, we bring both shuttles out to the ship where we will be helped by crew members of the *Treasure*. The first shuttles will carry just crew and food for the afternoon barbeques."

Dalmar studied him closely, looking for a chink of some kind in Ani's personal armor.

"Good. I will leave you one man per boat and the rest of us will wait on the island. Ani, I could use a smart guy like you in the future. Although you may become wealthy from this operation, I can offer you untold riches if you join my crew." Dalmar touched him on the shoulder. "Think about it. You have a bright future if you stick with me."

Ani stared ahead into the wind. "What will you do to them?" he asked.

"You mean the two men already on the island?" asked Dalmar. "What do you think I will do? What do you think?" he said through his trademark toothy grin.

The pirates arrived at the OAR Cay docks shortly before six a.m. Just as Ani had said, two men greeted them. The two were surprised for a moment at the number of people on the shuttle boats, and then they were both dead. The bodies were dragged and placed behind an old storage shed to the right of the dock and covered with palm leaves. Two of Dalmar's men went back to the ship on the shuttles — Dalmar sent Erasto with Chill and Taban went with Ani. Dalmar and the rest of the crew sat down in the storage shed and waited. The real operation had begun.

CHAPTER TWENTY-NINE

The *Treasure of the Seas,* anchored a quarter mile from OAR Cay, sat majestically on an angle balanced between the rising sun and the beach that would soon be occupied by passengers. Cabanas and beach chairs sat silently anticipating the day's crowds. Waves gently caressed the sand while gulls did their quick-step looking for food along the shore. The calmness of this most beautiful spot would soon be obliterated by vacationers that, not understanding its true beauty, would overrun it to reap every moment of benefit they could from their over-priced vacations.

On a shuttle making its way to the cruise ship, Ani contemplated his next move. If he went along with this he would be an accomplice to a horrible crime, or he would be dead and no one would know that he was innocent. If he tried to jump Taban, he would also end up dead. If he somehow managed to make it onto the ship and tried to tell someone of the plot, he would most assuredly not be believed. His best bet was to go along with the plan and wait until the right moment to try an escape.

Aboard the *Treasure of the Seas*, Cullen Nickels had been up for hours. He stared at the ceiling and walls and then finally got up and sat on the balcony. It was really just a matter of time now. He was caught. There was a good chance he would be leaving the ship in hand cuffs if he couldn't think of a brilliant way to explain himself. Elaine had already decided they would stay on board today. She intended to keep an eye on her weasel. They would remain in the room and order room service, they would talk about their marriage, and she would tell him that she'd known about him all along. It was better this way. It was better to have things out in the open. She wondered if her complicity made her the same kind of monster as her husband but decided, again, that it didn't.

Down the corridor, Jo and Jen spent much of the night

crying. Robby's temperature held steady at 102. The family

had so looked forward to exploring and enjoying the private

island, but it seemed they were locked in their room now,

and the mood had evaporated. This did not make Jo happy.

She thought that laws were almost certainly being broken in

the way her family was being treated and, if she wasn't so

embarrassed, she'd probably make a bigger stink. Jo was

extremely disappointed in her daughter. Clearly, based on

the pictures Drago had shown her, her angel of a daughter

had stolen the necklace. That was something she was

prepared to live with, didn't every kid do stuff like that at

some point? But making up the incredible story about Mr.

Nickels killing somebody, so Jen could throw the blame

somewhere else, that really bothered Jo. She thought she had

taught her daughter better. So, to some degree, she was

disappointed in herself, as well. Owning up to one's

mistakes figured hugely in her parenting style, but apparently it had not taken with Jen. She wondered again if she really stared at only the tip of the iceberg with her teenage daughter. Could this all be because of the divorce? Was she about to be bombarded with other teenage girl problems — the ones it appeared she had avoided with her good daughter? Would they both need years of therapy to solve this one?

Jo closed her eyes again and tried to sleep but couldn't.

The familiar sound of Jen's phone buzzing the arrival of a new text broke the silence. Jen groggily rolled over and then sat straight up in bed, startled by a thought that had slipped her mind for the last twelve hours. She grabbed her phone.

Just checking in to see how things are going.

"Mom. Mom, are you awake?"

"Yes dear, what is it? Is your father texting?"

"No. I mean, yes, he's texting, but that's not important. Mom, I know you don't believe me about what I saw yesterday."

Jo cut her off, "Honey, I just don't know what to believe."

"Listen to me for a second! I've got pictures! I forgot all about them when Captain Lover Boy and Drago the Torturer were grilling me, but I took pictures of the murder with my phone…here, look!"

She jumped out of bed and huddled over the phone with her mother, the many-hued light giving them an eerie pallor. Jo saw five pictures shot from a great distance. In the first, a man overpowered another from behind. In the second image, the attacker had lifted the other off the ground and held him by some sort of circle-shaped thing around the fellow's neck. The aggressor wore a black t-shirt, and Jo could not identify him. *Nickels?*

The pictures were compelling, but not proof positive that Nickels had committed a crime. However, the images demonstrated, as far as Jo was concerned, that her daughter hadn't lied about having seen a crime committed that day.

Jen said somberly, "I took the necklace. I don't know why I did it. I don't know what came over me and I'm sorry for putting you through this. But the necklace has nothing to do with the murder. Even though everyone wants to believe I'm a liar, I did *not* make up the murder to cover for taking the necklace…"

CHAPTER THIRTY

By nine in the morning, large numbers of passengers made their way to deck two and the gangplank to the shuttle boats. The line of eager tourists went part way down the hall, then curled up several flights of stairs and reached all the way to deck five. Some passengers lingered over breakfast so they wouldn't have to deal with standing on line. Others lounged on the deck, in no hurry to get off the ship. A few stragglers would stay aboard because they had no interest in the private island or because they preferred relative isolation, avoiding crowds of people jamming OAR Cay. The cruise line wanted to encourage passengers to explore their prize island, so the crew shut down shipboard amenities. The mall was closed, as were the casino, the pizzeria, mini-golf, and most of the bars. Minimal food options remained for those who could not be persuaded to leave. Jo, Jen, and Robby resigned themselves to staying. Robby's temperature simmered at the critical level of 103.

For members of the crew this was not the best day to have as a day off. Rather than be stuck hanging out in quarters too small to spend time in, most of the crew was scheduled for duty while the ship lay in OAR Cay. If you worked maintenance you cleaned decks, washed windows, vacuumed carpets, painted, or handled general cleanup. Most wait staff and kitchen staff went ashore and helped prepare meals or maintain outdoor seating areas. Some office staff was assigned to small shops set up to entice passengers with more t-shirts and trinkets they didn't need but purchased anyway. Others acted as lifeguards or helped in the clinic with inevitable cuts, bruises, and stings.

Captain Gunnar had intended to relax and read in his cabin, but he called a meeting of top staff for eleven a.m. He had several issues to discuss including the weather for the rest of the journey, a few security issues, and employees

fraternizing with passengers. He was, of course, a culprit in

the latter and he wished to straighten out rumors and

innuendo floating around. He offered a blunt, straight

forward apology, letting the crew know that he had been

smitten, but stood strong, deciding against further

involvement. It was a lesson they should all learn — save

themselves and the company embarrassment.

****

Staff, carrying large trays filled with food and

supplies, began boarding shuttles at about seven a.m. The

day's planned buffet consisted of ribs that had been pre-

cooked, Jamaican chicken, sliced hams, burgers, hot dogs,

and fries. Workers also carried salads, slaws, and several

kinds of cakes and cookies. Bartenders brought cases of

liquor and beer and others brought cream to fill portable ice

cream machines. All in all, they'd need three full-load trips with each shuttle boat, a well-honed process completed just after eight a.m. leaving the crew waiting to assist passengers about forty-five minutes to prepare.

Like the *Treasure,* OAR Cay functioned as a small city. After investments of several years and several million dollars, the little island approximated a tourist's dream isle. Disembarking passengers exited the shuttle via a corridor designed to organize people for security checks on their way back to the ship. Most people, once through the corridor, headed to the far left where white sand beaches beckoned. Cabanas with individual umbrellas protected pale-skinned vacationers from the sun's tropical rays. Each time a ship docked, sun worshipers dashed madly to snag the best locations, usually closest to the crystal sea water.

Going to the right from the security corridor brought visitors to a spring-fed lagoon where the company had sunk small boats and artifacts. Visitors could rent snorkel equipment or purchase underwater cameras and, as in a scavenger hunt, they could search out items or specific kinds of tropical fish and cross them off a list the company provided. A useless prize, maybe a photograph, went to the person who identified the most items, and the whole process was profitable for OAR.

Straight ahead after exiting the corridor laid the heart of the island. First there was a playground with slides and swings. Behind that, was the clinic, where the ships' doctor would set up for the day. Slightly to the left, guests enjoyed a spacious covered area with rows upon rows of picnic tables. Before long, enticing smells wafted from buffet lines behind the tables. A backdrop of giant palm trees divided this al fresco dining area from the adult-only beach at the other side of the island. A roped-off section in the water was designated for petting and feeding stingrays, for a fee, of course.

Guests rented bicycles, or played basketball, shuffleboard, horseshoes, and lawn darts. Less ambitious travelers chose peaceful seclusion in hammocks or shelled out more money to the massage staff.

The game was about money, and all along biking and walking paths photographers waited to take pictures of passengers at well-thought-out photo opportunity sites designed to be irresistible to lovers, families, singles, or anyone with cash in hand. One of the photographers, running late, caused the first problem of the day for Dalmar and crew. Ingmar Stevenson, on the ship for about two months, was last to get off the final shuttle. Sprinting toward his assigned rock formation photo-op on the farthest side of the island, he dropped a handful of cards he would hand out to passengers. Bending to pick them up, he glimpsed a pair of feet sticking out from behind a storage shed. Curiosity trumped lateness, so he sauntered over for a closer look.

From his perch in the shed, Dalmar watched the young man. When the photographer was about ten feet away, Dalmar motioned to Nadina Hanad. *Intercept the intruder.* Ingmar noticed the woman's long, tanned, muscular legs topped off by tight, white shorts as she strode toward him. She waived muscular arms, shown off by a uniform top a size too small for her Amazon frame.

"This area is for management staff only," she shouted. Ingmar was genuinely stopped in his tracks by her stunning physical appearance, but then he continued his approach.

"I'm sorry, I didn't know," he said, flashing his trademark grin. "I saw someone's feet behind the shed, so I thought I'd check it out." He continued to move in the direction of the bodies, which thoroughly pissed Nadina off. Why couldn't he just turn and get the hell out of here?

"I say again. This area is restricted. Now please turn around and go back."

Ingmar stopped. He took a long look at Nadina but couldn't place her. Surely, he would remember a fellow employee as physically imposing as she. "I'm sorry again. I haven't met you. I'm relatively new with the ship. My name is Ingmar. What's yours?" He stuck out a hand, offering to shake hers.

Nadina sighed to herself, realizing this wouldn't end well for Ingmar, attractive as he might be. "Alright," she said to him, bestowing a sexy smile. "You got me. A few of us are having a little party in the shack and well, I guess you're invited now. Do you like to party, Ingmar?"

He took a moment to consider the proposal, his eyes roving up and down her legs, then appreciating her well-endowed chest. He daydreamed for a moment about who else might be inside and thought briefly that the risk might lead him into the experience of his life. "Nah. I mean, yes, I like to party, but I've got to be at my assignment and I'm already late."

But Nadina had reached Ingmar, and she began to stroke his arm as she led him to the door of the shed. "Don't worry, baby. Nobody has to know," she whispered, rubbing against him.

She pulled him through the rickety door. *Could I get any luckier?* He thought.

Ingmar's throat seized up when his eyes adjusted to the dim interior light and he saw Dalmar and crew staring at him. He closed his eyes, totally aware that his curiosity and his lust had precipitated the last and greatest mistake of his very short life.

CHAPTER THIRTY-ONE

In the early morning hours, Jo came to realize with certainty that Robby did not have food poisoning. Clearly, the doctor couldn't diagnose or treat whatever he did have. Still, that doctor had medical experience and she needed some kind of help, right now. She picked up the phone and dialed the clinic. She also decided to text her ex-husband and she prayed for a quick reply.

Things not going well. I need your help. Robby is very ill. Can't rely on the ship's doctor.

Desiree Bronstad, a nurse from Norway, took Jo's call and decided to send a stretcher to bring Robby down to the clinic. Nurse Bronstad figured it was past time to supervise the boy in the medical area. She'd been watching and listening, well aware that Dr. Trainon's skill left much to be desired. The boy was in trouble and she would do what she could to help. The nurse called Dr. Trainon's room to wake him so he could meet the child and mother at the clinic. She

listened to five rings. No answer. She let it ring twenty-five

more times and then slammed the handset down and called

for a security officer to find Trainon. Meanwhile, two

security guards manning a stretcher picked Robby up and,

with Jo right behind; they carefully carried him to the clinic.

Jen remained in the room.

At the same time, another member of the security

team searched the employee cafeteria for Dr. Trainon. He

was nowhere to be found. The man took out his walkie-

talkie and called the security command center, asking them

to page the doctor. Again, no reply. Another member of the

thinning security team was sent to Trainon's cabin.

During the night, Dr. Trainon sat reflecting deeply

about the consequences of his potential misdiagnosis. He

should have checked the boy into a hospital in St. Thomas,

and his hesitation might now be life threatening. His career might be officially over. Kaput. Even so, he was tired of pretending. He was tired of being scared. He was tired of faking his way through everyday life. Seeking a way out, the best way out, he mixed a lethal cocktail of choice drugs (at least his medical knowledge afforded him the ability to do that) and inserted a needle into his arm around midnight. He left no note.

The security guard who found the body called nurse Desiree as Robby was carried into the clinic. She stood with her mouth open as she received the news.

"Where's the doctor?" Jo snarled.

Nurse Desiree froze with fear — how could she tell this mother that the doctor was dead? She steeled herself and walked calmly over to Robby. She readied a thermometer and put it into his mouth, then lifted his shirt and touched his abdomen. The skin was swollen, inflamed, and hard. Robby groaned when she touched it.

Jo said, in a sterner voice, "We need the doctor *now!*"

Her phone beeped — her husband responding.

What can I do? Give me some info.

"Nurse, I don't want to get crazy here, but where in the hell is the damned doctor?"

"Ma'am, your son is having an appendicitis attack."

"Where the hell is the doctor?" Jo screamed.

Desiree shook her head, "Listen, ma'am, I'm all you've got right now. You're going to have to trust me."

"Trust you! I don't know who you are. Where — is — the — *doctor*? Is he drunk or something?"

"No, ma'am, the doctor is dead," Nurse Desiree finally shouted back. "I'm all you've got, and we're going to figure out how to save your son."

"What do you mean save my son? What's going on?"

Desiree moderated her tone, hoping to calm the woman facing her, "In an appendicitis attack, when the temperature peaks it could mean the appendix has burst. If so, we're going to have to get a helicopter here right away, or I'll have to perform emergency surgery."

"You must be kidding." Jo shot back, still unglued. "Call a damn helicopter. There is *no* way you are going to cut my son open."

"I'll call, but it might be too late to transport him. We'll get through this, I promise. Let me help."

Jo's phone beeped.

What the hell is going on? Talk to me!!!

Nurse Desiree, glad of a momentary distraction of the mother, called the Captain to request a helicopter. Jo texted back to her husband.

Robby is having appendix attack. They might have to operate on him. They are incompetent! The doctor is dead. I don't know what to do!

CHAPTER THIRTY-TWO

The two shuttle boats pulled alongside and the crew

tethered them to the *Treasure of the Seas.* The first five or so

workers in the loading area could not figure out why shuttle

boats that were supposed to stay at the island were

returning to the ship. In an instant, all of Dalmar's crew was

aboard *Treasure* and Drago Stevinski appeared. Dalmar

greeted him and shook his hand as *Treasure's* crew members

watched in astonishment. After Dalmar whispered

something into Drago's ear, Drago called the

communications room on his walkie-talkie.

"This is **Treasure of the Seas Chief Security Officer** Drago.

Please put this message over the ship's intercom right now.

All security personnel are to report immediately to the

gangplank area on deck two. No exceptions. I repeat; all on

and off-duty security personnel report immediately to the

gangplank area on deck two. This is Chief Security Officer Drago."

Dalmar nodded and they waited. In the conference room Captain Gunnar, who was in his casual clothes and had asked his staff to dress likewise, had just started his meeting. He was sipping on a cup of hot tea when he heard Drago's announcement.

"What the hell is going on? Somebody get me a walkie-talkie and find out what this is about."

The phone in the conference room rang at the same time someone handed Captain Gunnar a walkie-talkie. Those in the room chose to let the phone ring while they kept their attention on the captain. Nurse Desiree's first call for permission to authorize a helicopter went unanswered.

"This is Captain Gunnar — what's going on Drago?"

There was a long pause as Drago contemplated his response.

"Drago — this is Captain Gunnar!"

"I'm sorry, sir," Drago said. "I am conducting an exercise. No need for alarm."

"An exercise? Why don't I know about it?"

"Sir, I needed to maintain secrecy to, er, test my team's response time."

Unused to having his authority usurped, the Captain felt his temper rise. "When you get your team's *response time,* come to the conference room…I will test *your* response time."

Dalmar nodded at Drago again. He asked, "Mr. Drago, is all of your security team assembled?"

"Yes, I believe they are."

"Gentlemen, may I have your attention?" Dalmar asked, addressing the ship's security people.

"We are conducting an anti-terrorism drill. I ask, for the purposes of this drill, that you secure these tie wraps on each other's wrists like so." He showed them, placing one of the ties on Drago's wrists, binding them together and tightening the tie until Drago squeaked a little. "It could hurt a little, but that's okay."

When he was satisfied that all the men were tied, he asked Drago to have them jump in the water, something they had done before in training. Most cruise lines test their employees in the water for various survival drills, but never with their hands bound by tie wraps. His men, intensely loyal and trusting, asked no questions. All jumped, except for Drago. To his astonishment, Dalmar, standing behind him, shoved hard and Drago ended up in the water with the others. The few seconds he was under water were the longest of his life, but by the time he surfaced he had convinced himself that Dalmar throwing him in the water was part of the ruse. One man, bobbing up right next to him, looked questioningly at his superior, seeking guidance.

"Sir, is this a drill or are we really in some sort of trouble?"

They both looked up at Dalmar's deadly face. As Drago dejectedly sunk his face into the ocean, his man stared at him, horrified.

"Drago, what have you done? Have you killed us all?"

Above, on Dalmar's nod, his men opened fire on those in the water. Bullets, pounded into the water for thirty seconds. The shooters paused for five seconds, and barraged for another ten. The attack left only a crimson sea and a moment of eerie quiet, broken when gulls swooped in to feed on scattered body parts shredded by bullets. Soon, the birds' white feathers were stained an uneven pink.

Distant, insistent gunfire briefly drew the attention of passengers playing and sunning on the beach at OAR Cay. The beach faced the ship, and many revelers stopped what they were doing to peer across the water, unable to decide at

such a distance if there was danger. Within a few moments,

their curiosity passed, and all went back to their vacations,

thinking nothing of it, a few figuring there would be

fireworks after sunset.

CHAPTER THIRTY-THREE

From their rooms, both Cullen and Jen heard the gunfire. To Jen, like those people on the beach, it just sounded like a fireworks celebration, but Cullen recognized gunfire when he heard it. Curiosity got the better of both of them and each went out on the balcony. Their rooms looked out the back of the ship, so neither could see what was happening around the sides. Jen climbed as high as she could and craned her neck to the right while balancing on the railing, but she saw nothing amiss. Turning back to her left, she flinched at the sight of Cullen Nickels two balconies over. He stared at her. A shiver snaked from her ankles, up through her spine, and into the back of her head. She lost her balance, teetered, but quickly recovered.

"Everything okay over there?" Cullen called.

Jen hurried inside without answering and locked the sliding door. The room suddenly felt constricting, as though it were shrinking. She searched for a way out other than through the glass doors or past the guard out front.

Realizing she had no options, Jen decided she might flirt with the two goons outside her door for a few minutes and then out-sprint them. But then, this ship left little choice for escape. And what was she running from, exactly? By the time those thoughts flitted across her mind, she had opened the door only to realize that there was no one positioned outside of it anymore. Well, she could just walk away, and she intended to, until Cullen Nickles opened his door.

Again, Jen slammed her door and leaned against the inside. She took quick, short breaths as she heard Cullen's unhurried footsteps coming closer. She jumped half a foot when he spoke through the door. She felt as if his lips were pressed right against her back.

"Wait, Jen. I just want to talk to you. Just for a moment. Please." Cullen pressed his ear against the door and could make out Jen's heavy breathing on the other side.

"Listen," he said, "I don't know what you think you saw yesterday, but it wasn't me. I can assure you, whatever you *think* you saw, you were mistaken."

Jen stood silent, frozen with fear. Her eyes darted around the room, seeking an escape. Cullen persisted at the door. *Why wouldn't he go away? Go away!*

"Please talk to me. Think about this. You are not only going to ruin your life and reputation, you'll ruin mine, as well!"

You should have thought of that before you practically twisted that guy's head off, Jen thought.

"I won't let you do that. Do you hear me in there?" he pounded on the door now, pretense gone, making no effort to speak quietly. "You will *not* smear my good name, girl!"

He rattled the knob and Jen almost wet herself as the door jiggled against her back.

From where she stood, knees knocking, she could see into the room's tiny closet. Scanning every inch of that last possible hope, certain it couldn't possibly offer a hiding place, she noticed one smooth panel in the closet ceiling dipping slightly askew and she saw an open space above. Jen jumped across four feet of carpet and into the closet, tossing out clothes and life jackets in her way. She ran her hands along the panels that made up the ceiling and realized she could push the panel up and dislodge it. Looking up, she made out a tangle of cables in the darkness, but she knew she'd found her escape route.

Unaware of the true seriousness of his family's plight aboard the ocean liner, Steve Sampson slammed his cell phone onto the desk and almost growled. After exchanging frantic text messages with his ex-wife and feeling helpless, he decided what he had to do. A block away from his

veterinary clinic was the office of his friend, Dr. Mike Menti.

Menti, a general surgeon, would know what to do once he

heard Robby's symptoms. Slapping his baseball cap onto his

head, Steve bounded down the stairs and had his car in gear

almost before he sat down. A moment later, tires squealing,

he skidded to a stop in Mike's parking lot and sprinted for

the office. Unconcerned about anything but his family, he

dashed to the receptionist's window, slid the glass divider

roughly aside, and hollered, "I need to see Mike, *now!*"

The receptionist stared over her glasses at him,

glanced to the patients waiting, looked back at him, and then

to the patients again. She pushed the appointment list and a

pencil at him with shaking hands and tried to respond

politely.

"Sir, please, sign the check-in list. If you don't have an

appointment…"

Steve growled again, "No! I am a colleague of Mike's. I need his help with an urgent matter."

"Sir, I can't put you ahead of all of these people…"

Steve had had enough. He leaned past the silly woman and yelled, *"Mike! Mike!* It's Steve Sampson — I need your help right away!" He shouted through the receptionists' window into the offices behind. When she tried to close the window, Steve stuck his hand in front of it and stopped her.

Dr. Menti had just finished with a patient and Steve's yelling brought him into the reception area in time to see the receptionist stand and threaten to call the police.

Mike stayed her hand and addressed his friend, "Steve, what on earth?"

"Buzz me back. I have a medical emergency."

Shrugging, Mike patted his receptionist's shoulder and pushed the buzzer to unlock the door. He put his arm around Steve and escorted him back into his office. "All

right, buddy, relax. Chill. You know I can't help you with

dogs and cats, right?"

CHAPTER THIRTY-FOUR

Fifteen minutes later, Steve texted Jo.

Have the nurse call the following number. I am standing by with a surgeon friend of mine.

Within a few minutes Nurse Desiree connected with Dr. Menti, and they began a dialogue.

"Nurse, when you apply pressure to his abdomen, is the pain worse when you press down or when you release?" Nurse Desiree touched the boy's abdomen, pressing and releasing.

"His pain is worse when I release," she said.

"Do you have a white cell count?"

"No doctor, we don't have a lab, and I just got involved this morning. Our doctor committed suicide last night."

Menti put his hand over the phone and turned to Steve. "What the heck is happening on that ship?"

Uncovering the phone, he spoke again to Desiree, "Okay. How long have the symptoms persisted. What's his temperature?"

"The mother says he's been vomiting for several days and his temperature is 103.8 right now."

"How long before you could get a helicopter, nurse?"

"I've been trying to raise the Captain to get permission, but I can't reach him. Based on where we are, I would expect we could get a medical helicopter here within an hour, if it was approved."

"Approved?" Menti snapped, but then moderated his voice and spoke authoritatively, but without rancor. "I'm approving it! Now listen, you have one hour, tops, to get that helicopter out there or you'll be performing your first surgery. Do you understand what I'm saying? I'm not willing to wait any longer than sixty minutes. Ok, I'm going to let you go and make that happen. You will call me back in no more than fifteen minutes with an update. Now move!"

They hung up. Pale, but determined, Nurse Desiree grabbed the phone and called in another page for her captain.

Gunnar, still dressed in his casual clothes, had decided to go down to check on Drago. The phone rang again in the conference room, and again, he ignored it as he walked out. In all his years, he'd never heard of a drill like Drago described, and certainly not when a ship was in an active cruise mode. Lately, Drago's behavior was perplexing. The fellow had been under pressure from home, apparently, but Gunnar had no idea how great the pressure was, or its source.

Drago's family were tobacco farmers in his native Bulgaria, and had been for generations. They'd wanted him to join the family business but though an astute businessman, Drago had little interest in tobacco. For as long

as he could remember, his passion was police work and he

enlisted in the Bulgarian Navy at eighteen without his

parents knowing. He thought he could jump start himself

into policing. After a few years in the Navy, he returned to

the farm with a new wife and a child. His brood quickly

grew to four children. Drago forced himself to struggle with

the family business, but opportunity knocked and he

answered. He jumped on an opening with the local police,

and his career took off like a jack rabbit with its tail on fire,

until an incident altered his and his family's paths for good.

His police captain made a habit of accepting bribes.

Although Drago never took a dime, he knew about the

money, and so, implicated, had had to resign. Wallowing in

shame, his extended family pitched him off the farm and out

of their lives. His wife and children remained on the farm.

Six months out of work, and he landed his first job on a

cruise ship — a member of the security team. He did well and moved from cruise line to cruise line, earning promotions right up to Chief Security Officer on the *Treasure of the Seas.*

Over the past few years he had reconciled with his father and mother but not with his brother who'd taken over the farm and nearly lost it. Failure to keep up with the times forced the farm into bankruptcy. Keeping it afloat and in the family was more difficult by the day. Somewhere in this mire of misfortune, Drago's youngest child developed a cancerous tumor, and Drago's cruise line salary failed to cover expenses. Drago, desperate, explored any angle to make a few extra dollars, beginning with supervising the occasional sale of pilfered cruise line equipment or food on the black market.

He met Korfa Osman in his black market dealings. Money poured in and Drago envisioned saving the farm and his child. Korfa suggested Drago's expertise as Chief Security Officer on the *Treasure of the Seas* might be a goldmine.

"Hey," Korfa said, slapping Drago's shoulder affably, "they will take a few rich passengers as hostages and only when they are off the ship on excursions. Your hands won't get dirty, my friend. You just alert my associates as to who has money and when they will be off the ship. Simple."

Reluctant at first, Drago began to cave in to Korfa's goading. He saw himself making the final score to set his family free from debt and danger. He never suspected that the huge OAR ship was the real target, or that crew and passengers would be murdered. He also never expected to find himself floating face down in a sea of red.

On the *Treasure,* with Drago and company disposed of, Dalmar's crew began their assignments. Doratai took Amina to guest relations to make the planned announcements. As soon as they commenced, others would clear the decks and herd those remaining aboard into designated areas.

Captain Gunnar, making his way down the stairs, heard the first announcement made by a beautiful, melodic voice like something off a radio station introducing cool jazz. The voice was compelling, the message convincing, but the problem was he'd never heard this particular voice before.

"Attention passengers of the Treasure of the Seas that have stayed aboard with us while your fellow travelers visit our private island. This is a special anniversary cruise for the OAR line. Those remaining onboard today will receive complementary passes for a free cruise to be enjoyed at your leisure! Ladies and gentlemen, there are no strings attached. This is our gift to you for joining us on our special day. All guests onboard please report to the Aqua Lounge Theater, on deck four, to claim your reward. I repeat, all

guests' onboard report to the Aqua Lounge Theater on deck four to

claim your prize of a free cruise on the Treasure of the Seas!"

Gunnar stopped in his tracks. *Ridiculous. Had someone*

broken into the radio room to play a prank? No matter what this

was about, Gunnar would be stuck explaining it to ticked-off

vacationers showing up to collect their free cruises. His

anger level ramped up one more notch.

Doratai flicked a switch so Amina's next

announcement went only to decks one and two where the

crew was located.

"All staff members currently onboard. Please report

immediately to the ice rink on deck three. This is a mandatory call

for all staff currently onboard, regardless of what task you may

currently be performing. Report immediately to the ice rink. This

mandatory meeting is about bonuses each of you will receive to

send home to family and loved ones. This is a priority-one meeting.

All staff, no matter their current assignments, must report to the skating rink in five minutes."

As Amina repeated each message several times and in several languages, the rest of the pirates attacked their jobs. Erasto and Taban started on the bottom two decks and directed stray employees to the ice rink. Ghadi and Kader worked their way up from deck three. Nadina Hanad sprinted up to eight in a trance-like fury.

CHAPTER THIRTY-FIVE

Desiree Bronstad was trapped in the most horrific fifteen minutes of her already horrific life. Despite the air-conditioning tickling her face, she felt a bead of sweat trickle down the back of her white cotton uniform. She'd gotten into nursing because she thought it a noble and worthy profession. Her father was a fisherman and her mother a school teacher in their small town in Norway. They were proud when she decided to get into nursing and even prouder when she'd gotten a job on a cruise ship. Her father was especially happy that she would ply her trade where, he said, "his family that was born of the sea, was most comfortable living their lives."

What her father didn't know was that, although his daughter had gotten her nursing certificate, she had barely passed the tests and lived with a horrible reputation of not being able to tolerate the sight of blood. Her classmates called her *Sykepleir Spy* — Nurse Vomit.

The first time she puked, no one thought much of it. Most medical students get queasy or lose their lunch when they start out, but by the third and fourth instance, Desiree was worried. Then came the day she started to draw blood from a patient, found the room spinning, passed out, and crumbled to the floor. The needle stuck straight up in her frightened patients arm, wobbling slightly. It seemed to be the last straw. She wondered how a girl that had grown up watching her father gut fish, the odor of sea and slime still stuck in her nostrils, could keel over every time she saw blood. Eventually, she controlled her gag reflex and stopped vomiting, but she was unable to convince instructors that she was worthy of a letter of recommendation. Thus, Nurse Vomit ended up on the *Treasure of the Seas* for the past two years. Her duties covered a profusion of colds, sprains, hangovers, and food poisoning. She'd occasionally treated

minor cuts and scrapes, but never any gushing blood. Now,

she held a phone in her hand and reached out for someone

in authority to give her an okay to get a helicopter, while she

searched the medical supply room for surgical supplies. If

the helicopter didn't arrive, there would be a profusion of

blood this day.

"Please pick up the phone, Captain," she mumbled to

herself as she let the phone ring on a continuous loop. She

hung up and called different numbers on the list beside the

phone. She tried the Captain's line; no answer. Then she

tried the Chief Security Officer; no answer. Desperate, she

called the Cruise Director's office and even tried the

Executive Chef and the Children's Activity Director. No one

picked up.

At precisely the same moment that Nurse Desiree

decided to go on a quest for anyone of any authority, Erasto and Taban, engaged in clearing the lower decks, opened the clinic door.

"What are you still doing here?" asked Erasto. "Did you not hear the pages for all employees to gather at the ice rink?"

No, she had not heard the pages. The loud speaker system had long ago stopped working in the medical office, and no one had bothered to fix it. She had no clue who these two men were. "I have a medical emergency here and I won't be going anywhere right now!"

Neither Erasto nor Taban knew what to say; this was not in any contingency plan. One of them pushed the nurse aside and went into the back room where Robby lay, with his mom sitting beside his bed.

"Oh, thank God," said Jo, when Erasto and Taban came into the room. "Are you doctors? My son is seriously ill and I don't think the nurse can handle this. Please. Help us."

Erasto and Taban again exchanged glances, again confused. They about-faced and retraced their steps, checking out their surroundings and ignoring the two women while Jo yelled, "What's wrong? We need your help. Where are you going? Do you not understand English?"

Nurse Desiree stepped in front of the two men and said with more courage than she felt, "You both are to leave immediately. Get out. I'm going to have to perform surgery on that boy soon, and I'm not sure who you are, but I am sure you can't stay in here."

"Madam," answered Erasto, "you are in no position to dictate anything." He pulled his white uniform shirt up to reveal his pistol. "Now shut up. Put your hands behind your head and kneel on the floor." As Nurse Desiree sank to her knees, he motioned Taban to take out his walkie-talkie. "Call Dalmar and tell him what's going on."

"Wait," Taban said. "Let's think about this. You already know what Dalmar is going to tell us to do to them. It's a woman, and a sick kid-they won't cause us any problems."

Nurse Desiree began to find strength that she didn't know she had. She rose and turned toward her adversaries.

"Down!" Erasto yelled, sticking the pistol against her head.

"I will *not*. I am going in that room to take care of that boy. You do what you have to do, and I'm going to do what I have to do." She reached up and turned the barrel of the gun away from her head, then defiantly walked into the other room, silently praying, waiting to be shot in the back of the head.

Taban grabbed Erasto. "Let her do what she has to do, my friend. They can do no harm in here. Let's continue our job and clear the rest of the workers that are a legitimate threat to us. Listen to me," he grabbed a padlock he saw on the counter. "We can lock the door from the outside, and forget them. Now let's go."

Erasto looked down and thought for a moment before he turned back towards the room. "You have to do what you have to do, and I have to do what I have to do," he said, glaring first at his partner then at Desiree.

He grabbed the cell phone from Jo's hand and smashed it on the floor, stomping the pieces. Scanning the room with his eyes, he saw the wall phone, stalked over, and ripped it from the wall. Turning to the two women and the child, he held them in his line of vision for a long moment. Both women were certain they faced death. He turned away and walked out of the room, locking the door from the

outside.

CHAPTER THIRTY-SIX

Captain Gunnar knew something was seriously

wrong as he raced down the stairs, but he did not

understand the depths of the situation until he saw the

hulking form of Nadina Hanad walking down the corridor

of deck eight with her AK-47. He ducked around a corner

and observed her with one eye as she looked at the piece of

paper in her hand and then at door numbers.

This much was clear, the ship was under some sort of

terrorist attack. Gunnar's Chief of Security was either in on

the plot or had been overtaken. He assumed the former,

based on the nonsense about conducting an exercise. Then,

again, that could have been the Chief's signal that something

was wrong. *Thank God*, Gunnar thought, *most of the*

passengers are off the ship.

He kept watching, with horror and disappointment in

his inability to unfreeze his limbs, as the woman with the

body of a male weight lifter pounded on a cabin door. An older man opened the door and then thrust himself back against it when he saw Nadina and her assault rifle. She grabbed his shoulder and shoved him into the room, now out of Captain Gunnar's view. He could hear the man say they weren't interested in a free cruise and then heard the man's wife yelling but could not make out her words. An instant later, two shots exploded and the muscle woman walked out the door. She noted something on the paper she pulled from her back pocket.

Fear pulsed through Gunnar exactly as it had when his brother was shot. His body was still paralyzed, but his mind raced, seeking an escape. *How could this be happening? His ship was under attack.* In nautical school this sort of thing was never mentioned. No one thought such a take-over possible or even likely.

Now, Gunnar focused on action. *Attempt to disarm the muscle woman?* He was sure he couldn't over power her, nor could he expect to get the gun away from her. He thought about how he had distained the whole *Captain must go down with his ship* thing, realizing he stood smack in the middle of such a scenario. If he did not try to be a hero, and he escaped somehow, he would be a laughing stock or face high criticism. If he got killed in an act of heroism, he'd rest in peace — but dead is dead. He remembered something an instructor had said about there being no such thing as a dead hero. One thing he had going for him was that he was dressed in civilian clothes and, with that thought he knew what he must attempt to do.

Thinking of the earlier announcement requesting passengers to gather in the Aqua Lounge Theater, Gunnar figured he might have a chance to see what was happening if he lost himself among other guests. He headed for the

Aqua Lounge, stopping at the purser's office near guest

relations on deck five.

The Pursers office was one of the nicest behind the

scene places on the ship. It had recently been refurbished in

an old-fashioned nautical style. Rich blues and deep golds

set off new black leather couches and chairs. A thick carpet

woven with pictures of navigational tools used throughout

history cushioned the floor and impressively framed,

oversized photographs of the OAR Fleet's twenty-three

ships hung side-by-side around the walls. Facing the door,

there was a guilt framed portrait of the grandson and

current president of the company, James Billington III,

sitting on the edge of his gigantic Victorian desk.

Captain Gunnar remembered meeting Billington III

once at an event held at Billington's estate and attended by

company big wigs and ship captains who were not at sea.

He seemed a gracious host and a respectable man, but

beyond that Gunnar wasn't impressed. In fact, in the few minutes that they spoke, OAR's president came across as not very intelligent. Gunnar thought good fortune played more of a part in the guy's success than anything else had.

Gunnar remembered that one of the Billington daughters, Marina, showed up quite inebriated. She kept offering guests free cruises, preening because *she* owned the boats. She ended up putting her hand in a bowl of cocktail sauce and knocking it and the giant shrimp bowl to the floor.

"Daddy," she slurred, "you gonna needs jest a wee bit more shrimps!" Her father busied himself with other guests as an employee escorted Marina into the main house.

Dismissing that thought, Gunnar entered a small room in the pursers' office called the *Marina Room*. It contained a few safety deposit boxes for passengers' use and a large one for the Captain. Gunnar's box held a bit of foreign currency, his college ring, a much younger picture of him with Sophia Caltimano, and a tiny Beretta 3032 Tomcat handgun with an extra seven-round magazine. He separated the gun and the magazine already attached, putting the ammo into his left pocket. He stuffed the second magazine into his right pocket. Removing his wallet and identification from his back pocket, he stowed them in the safety deposit box and bent to conceal the gun in his left sock. Gunnar was as ready as he could be to defend his ship.

CHAPTER THIRTY-SEVEN

Jen crawled blindly through the blackness of the

airspace above her room, feeling cables and not much else in

her way. She wrinkled her face at the musty dustiness and

rubbed her nose every few seconds as she moved

deliberately forward on hands and knees while her eyes

adjusted to the darkness. She was in duct work connecting

rooms to the hallway. She decided her only option was to

keep going, exploring, though the confined space

intimidated her. As she moved along, she felt the tin walls

charge at her in a claustrophobic sprint for her senses. She

felt caged. Her eyes rolled back as she flashed to memories

of her first pet. Her father, ever eager to share his love of

animals, had gotten her a clownfish. She named the creature

Nemo and watched it for hours as it swam alone in the

tropical home she had created for it. She recognized that the

fish was trapped all alone in a tiny cylinder, but she loved how it glided and moved and looked happy to be swimming and breathing.

Her own breathing quickened, her claustrophobic response deepening, and she remembered the day she removed her pet from the water. She watched his body expand and contract as his gills sought oxygen laden water, not dry air, and he struggle to survive. She casually put the pad of her index finger on his flesh and covered his gills until he breathed no more. Then she cupped him in her hands and gently placed him back in his bowl, first watching him sink to the bottom and then mesmerized as he slowly floated to the surface.

The memory of Nemo, like so many other childhood memories, seemed locked in a section of her mind that was opening itself to her little by little. As the walls of the air condition duct inched ever closer, Jen recalled how her fathers' great trust in her had led to her being put in charge of the veterinary clinic's adoptive program when she was thirteen. She cared for sick and injured kittens and helped countless numbers find adoptive homes. Those that could not be adopted were eventually sent to a pound. She found a different solution for others when she couldn't bear to see them suffer. Like little Pueblo, who suffered from vertigo and had an inoperable tumor on his throat. *Poor helpless thing.*

From a deep, dark, secret vault of her mind, she called up the day she had solved Pueblo's problem. Knowing the little fellow would never recover, Jen lovingly lowered the cat into a travel carrier and then slid the box into the back seat of her mother's car, where it then baked in ninety-five degree Florida sun.

Later, Jen watched from inside the house as her father removed the lifeless animal from its superheated car coffin, and she continued to watch him bury the body in a vacant lot next door. Her father didn't ask her for an explanation.

Jen recalled her parents talking between themselves about the death, but they never spoke to her of it. Over the years, she recalled visiting the burial site many times and visualizing the corpse of the cat buried deep in the earth, trying to draw breaths. She felt no guilt or remorse, quite sure the cat needed her help, needed release. After bulldozers arrived to clear the lot for new construction, Jen dropped the memory and moved on.

Her thoughts came back to her present predicament and she became aware again of her suffocating reality. Her own breathing paced itself back to normal. She thought back, with fascinated clarity, to the breath of the animals and how that process captivated her. She saw, again, the rhythmic fluid motion of their chests heaving up and down until they just stopped moving.

Feeling imprisoned in his cabin below, Cullen paced.

When his wife got up to go to the bathroom, he slipped out

the door and started to walk. Not sure where he was going,

he was certain something weird was up and he had to find

out what. He got about twenty feet down the hall before he

heard a sneeze. He looked around the hall, but felt sure the

sound originated above his head. The ceiling. Cullen looked

up, a slow smile spreading across his lips. *Well now.* He

could certainly take care of his little problem neighbor right

now, but he decided the situation on board, whatever it

might be, could put him in better shape than he'd originally

thought.

He moved on, past the spot where he knew Jen

crouched above him. A gunshot rang out far down the

corridor. Cullen startled for an instant, then, like a shadow,

glided into a small ironing closet for guest use. He stationed

himself in front of a pull-down ironing board, bending his

head to clear stray wire hangers dangling from a clothes bar. He left a small gap in the door and shut off the lights.

Peering from the darkness, something he was quite accustomed to doing, Cullen watched Ghadi and Kadar walk down the hall, each with an AK-47 strapped across his shoulder. As they approached and passed, he overheard their comments about two passengers unaccounted for in room 9504 and three in 9500. For the first time, Cullen Nickels felt like the prey. He did not like the feeling. Something big was going on here; these terrorists, or whoever they were, had boarded the ship and were collecting passengers. *Killing them?* At the moment, they aimed to collect Cullen and Elaine. A thought flashed across his mind. *Letting them kill Elaine might not be the worst thing.* She knew his secrets. She had ordered him to retire from his passion. *Couldn't this play out in his favor?* Conflicted, he couldn't figure out which way to lean. He loved her.

Another sneeze came from the ceiling. Ghadi and Kadar frowned at each other and then walked to the spot where the sound had originated. Jen froze, trying not to move a muscle.

"They must have pretty big rats on this ship, eh?" Ghadi said to Kadar.

"Yeah, so big they sneeze," Kadar guffawed and spit on the floor.

Jen tightened more, trying to make herself tiny, even invisible. Her toes cramped and her breath choked in her throat. .

"Now where do you think that rat is?" Ghadi pointed his rifle at the ceiling. "Right about…here." He moved a shoulder and aimed.

Cullen had to intervene. He came out of the room, carrying a pair of pants that had hung in the closet, and walked casually toward the two surprised men.

"Gee whiz, can somebody tell me how you work one of these things?" he asked, grimacing at the hot iron in his hand. Before either could react, Cullen threw the pants and smashed the scalding iron across each face. He booted one gun away, picked up the other, and shot Ghadi in the neck.

"Fifty-one. But who's counting?" he chortled as he walked over to Kadar, who had managed to get up on all fours. Cullen kicked in Kadar's ribs and jabbed a knee sharply into the pirate's back, pressing the hot iron down on his bare neck. Kadar shrieked and collapsed.

"Oh, come on now, it can't be that hot anymore. Think of it as a nice warm cruise ship massage." He leaned down, close to Kadar's ear, and spoke again in deadly calm tones.

"Listen, asshole, I don't know what the hell is going on here, but you're about to tell me everything. Clear?"

Cullen turned Kadar over and centered the iron above his victim's eyes. "Are you some kind of terrorist?"

Kadar closed his eyes and did not answer.

"You know, in my country, mostly women do the ironing. You may not think I know how to handle one of these things, but since I retired, I got bored and learned new skills. Yep, I've gotten to do a lot of housework." Reaching back, he jammed the iron into Kadar's groin and closed his own eyes, relishing the scream of pain. "Who are you with, and how many of you are aboard?"

"I am not a terrorist. I am a pirate," Kadar managed to get out between heavy breaths. "There are fifty of us onboard. You cannot possibly stop us."

Cullen stood up and dragged Kadar by his hair into the ironing closet. He took Kadar's belt that held his walkie-talkie, a knife, and a pistol and buckled it on himself while Kadar, immobilized, watched. "What kind of gun is this? I'm not familiar with it?" Cullen asked. "Never mind." He fired

a shot between Kadar's eyes. "Whoops. My mistake. It's a

nine by nineteen millimeter Grand Power K100, Slovak

semi-automatic pistol with a seventeen round detachable

box magazine. Sound about right?"

Cullen stepped back into the hall and dragged the

other body into the closet, arranging both neatly next to each

other. He stepped out of the closet and pulled the door shut.

"Fifty-two," he said.

Cullen studied the area over his head to visualize

where Jen was hiding, having heard her scrambling while he

disposed of the bad guys. He nodded, opened the small door

again and then spoke to the ceiling in the closet.

"The way I look at it, you've got little choice but to

come out of there and stick with me. At least you might have

a chance of surviving." He waited, but got no response.

"Okay. You have it your way, but I'm planning on getting

off this ship alive, and frankly, if I'd wanted to I could have killed you by now."

Jen slid open a panel in the ironing closet ceiling and lowered herself down. Her tee-shirt was filthy, covered in fuzzy dust, and her hair was stuck together with sweat. She looked at the corpse's right next to her feet and at the blood on the floor. Cullen was impressed with two things. For the first time, he noticed and admired her agile teenage body, and he marveled that the girl had reacted not at all to blood and dead bodies. He wondered how much they might have in common.

"When should I expect that you're gonna do that to me?" she asked, nodding at the bodies.

Cullen looked her in the eye, "Why'd you follow me?"

"Don't know," she said. "Why'd you snap that guy's neck?"

Cullen smiled at her. "Listen, we make a deal. I get you off this ship alive and we forget about everything else that happened."

"Why should I trust you? I mean, how do I know you won't put a bullet in the back of my head and say one of them did it?"

"Because," came another voice, "you're not a derelict. You're not a drug addict or someone that won't be missed. That's the type he likes to kill, honey!" Elaine Nickels stepped into view behind Cullen. "And," she said, grabbing Jen in a protective bear hug, "Because I say he won't."

CHAPTER THIRTY-EIGHT

Dalmar entered the ice rink with Nadafi Tenge, Korfa Osman, and Doratai by his side. Employees sat in the seats surrounding the rink, though Dalmar had wanted them gathered on the ice. Shaking his head, he reached for his walkie-talkie.

"This is Dalmar. All check in now with status reports."

One by one he heard from each of his crew except for the deceased Ghedi and Kader. He turned and faced Doratai. "I need as accurate a count as possible — the number of employees in this room."

"Yes. I lost count at around three-hundred," she responded, shrugging.

"Count again. An accurate count, just like I said."

Doratai counted like her life depended on it — and it most assuredly did. In a few moments she came back with,

"There are three-hundred and twelve people in the room, sir. Seven unaccounted for."

"That's good. Tenge, get them all down to the rink." The escalating noise in the room irritated Dalmar. He could not hear himself think.

"What's this about a bonus?" a voice called out.

"Please, hurry this along. I've left my station and I need to return," hollered another.

Tenge looked around, drew his pistol, and fired a shot into the air. The room went as silent as a wake. "Everyone move down onto the ice."

A murmur of dissention brewed among the group, but they moved down to the ice where they stood silently as Erasto and Taban came into the rink.

"Ladies and gentlemen," Dalmar announced. "This is Erasto and Taban. They are here to provide you with your bonuses."

He motioned to the men and they complied with a barrage of rapid fire on the three hundred and some odd people. Chaos erupted as people figured out what was happening and began screaming. Short-lived chaos. They kept firing until the rink was a pool of blood. Some three hundred bodies lay on top of each other. None had suspected what was about to happen to them. The room quieted except for a few moans and the pirates opened fire again until no more sounds were heard.

"Now, why aren't Ghadi and Kadar responding?" Dalmar asked of Tenge, who then spoke into his walkie-talkie.

"Nadina, where are you? Have you heard from Ghadi and Kader?"

A crackle and hiss, and her voice came back, "I am currently on deck ten. Last I heard from them, they were just about to finish clearing nine."

"We have seven members of the crew unaccounted for, have you seen any?"

"Yes, I took out two cleaning people on deck eight, so that would leave five."

"Good," Dalmar cut in. "Tell her the rest are probably too scared to make a difference. She should go back to nine and find Ghadi and Kader. Then I want her to meet me on the bridge along with Amina. Korfa, you and Tenge take Doratai and get to the Aqua Lounge — you'll keep an eye on the remaining passengers."

Doratai, the Croatian girl assigned to deliver up-to-date passenger and employee manifests arrived on deck two with the information in her hands. Looking out into the water, she saw the pool of blood and her knees grew weak. She stumbled, making a short sound in her throat. Dalmar grabbed the papers and assured her she was far too valuable to end up in the water like the others. He led her to a chair and ordered her to explain the counts.

Doratai began cautiously, "Of the three thousand four-hundred and seventy-eight passengers, three thousand one-hundred and twenty-three passed through the scanners this morning to go to OAR Cay. That leaves three-hundred and fifty-five passengers onboard."

"Good. A manageable number," Dalmar responded.

Doratai continued, "Of thirteen hundred and fifteen employees, nine-hundred and eighty left the ship, with three-hundred and thirty-five remaining. Oh, minus one more. It appears our doctor expired by his own hand during the night." She looked into the water again. "I...I'm not sure how many we should minus that are out there."

"It's fifteen, plus the doctor — leaving three-hundred and nineteen aboard. Nicely done, young lady. I may be in need of your computer expertise again. Please, do not stray

far."

CHAPTER THIRTY-NINE

Luigi Santolini, the Maestro of Maître D's, enjoyed his day off. He especially loved days like this, when the ship was quiet and he could be alone practicing the accordion or playing the piano. Jerry Klondike, his most recent conquest, sat next to him on the piano stool. Jerry was better known as *Sir Jon Elton* on Mondays, Wednesdays, and Fridays and as *Joely Bill* on Tuesdays, Thursdays, and Saturdays. The two men sat as close as two hillbillies side-by-side in a pick-up truck — Luigi's left leg overlapped Jerry's and their heads touched gently.

Lost in their moment, they never heard the gunfire that preceded Nadina Hanad into the piano bar. Luigi slid his hand inside the waistband of Jerry's trousers, unaware that the hulking woman was coming up behind them. She laughed, at first to herself and then out loud, startling the two men. They jumped to their feet, Luigi momentarily getting his hand caught in Jerry's pants.

"Did you lover boys miss the announcements?" she said to them, displaying a sarcastic smile.

"What announcements?" Luigi stammered, his face as red as the silk shirt he had ready to wear that night.

"We were just practicing," Jerry said, sounding equally as flustered.

"You were supposed to meet with the other employees in the skating rink," she fired back. "Now, unfortunately, I will be forced to make a mess of your fine piano room."

Jerry assessed the situation, feeling instinct and terror kick in. He lowered his head and charged Nadina, who unloaded a torrent of gunfire into his chest. His momentum crashed him into her powerful legs and pushed her backwards giving Luigi just the daylight he needed to make a break. He sprinted out of the piano bar and onto the main

concourse of deck eight, Nadina in close pursuit. Luigi

zigzagged, again by instinct, to dodge her fire and get to the

library room. He dashed out the other side and leaped up

the stairwell, running for deck nine. Nadina, faster and more

powerful, pursued through the library and up the stairs,

pausing once or twice to listen for the out-of-shape and

panting Maître D to give away his direction. When he

reached the Internet center, Luigi dove under a table and

trembled, clueless about why he was being chased by this

super-woman soldier. His white, partially unbuttoned shirt

was soaked with sweat and stuck tightly to his soft, flabby

body. Fleetingly, he wished he had taken advantage of the

employee work out room.

From the doorway, Nadina scanned the Internet

center. Seeing nothing, she reversed to exit the way she had

come in, but Luigi, misjudging her direction and overcome

by terror, dove out from under the table and ran. A bullet tore through his left calf and came out the other side. His adrenaline spike covered the pain as he galloped, like a man possessed, down the hall and toward the back of the ship. He had never run this much in his life — it felt like his heart would tear through his chest. If he stopped, he would be shot or his heart would explode, so he hurtled forward, gaining speed until he reached an ironing room and rushed inside, closing the door behind him. Nadifa, not as familiar with the twists and turns of the ship's layout walked carefully but swiftly down the hall, upset with herself that she had allowed this girly man to elude her.

As Luigi tried desperately to catch his breath, he willed his eyes to adjust to the total blackness. He put his face against the wall for its coolness and thought it odd that his cheek felt wet. He touched his face with his hand and transferred the wetness. Unable to hold out any longer without knowing if he was bleeding, he reached along the

wall searching for a light switch, which he soon found. He

kept his finger on it for several moments as he contemplated

whether or not it was wise to turn it on. He flicked it on,

blinked like an owl, and flicked it off quickly. He flicked it

on again and gaped at two battered, bloodied bodies

belonging to Ghadi and Kader. An iron, layered with blood,

lay next to one of them. He didn't recognize the dead men

but didn't want to wait to figure out who they were. He

turned the light off.

Nadina watched the light turn on, off, on, off. She

smiled, just as Luigi burst from the room and took off to his

left. He reached the back of the ship and literally saw the

bullets smash into the door of 9504 as he raced around the

corner and back to the starboard side of the ship. As she

moved past the closet door, Nadina looked inside and saw

the bodies of her colleagues on the floor. She momentarily

mourned the loss of friends, then realizing she'd never liked them anyway, she shrugged and took off after Luigi.

Luigi made it back to the stairwell and two-stepped up to deck ten. He half-jumped, half-rolled over a counter and into a buffet area as another hail of Nadina's gunfire exploded around him. Crying and slobbering, he ran through an open door to the kitchen and crashed face-first into hanging pots and pans. The force of the crash landed him flat on his back, bloodying his head. Nadina stepped inside and hovered over the sweat-soaked and bleeding Luigi. She unholstered her knife and pointed it toward Luigi's panting mouth.

"What the hell are you? What did I do?" he begged, wheezing, and not really wanting answers. She drew back her knife to plunge it into Luigi's chest, but a timer rang on a nearby stove, distracting her just enough to allow him to muster the hardest punch he'd ever thrown in his life. It missed where he wanted it to land, but crashed squarely into

Nadina's elbow joint. For a brief moment her entire arm

went numb and the burn winged up her arm, making her

cry out and grab her elbow. Luigi, thanking all saints and

gods for crazy-bone reactions, pushed off and scrambled out

the other side of the kitchen.

"You are becoming a real pain!" she called out after

him, pursuing again. Luigi made it to the pool area and

jumped over beach chairs like a fat Olympic hurdler. He

grabbed his falling pants and willed himself a second wind.

Never slowing, Luigi stared ahead at the pool slides, seeing

the transparent plastic ends and the dark yellow opaque

middle section. He had a plan. Reaching the stairwell for the

pool slide, he climbed it at top speed, amazed that he hadn't

keeled over yet.

He would slide partially down into the opaque part of

the tube, where he would hang, hidden from view, for as

long as he could. With one fell swoop, he launched down the slide, fighting his own body weight pushing him toward the bottom. His hands burned against the tube as he frantically clutched at the walls to slow his dissent. He dug in with ragged fingernails, ripping at the plastic and brought himself to a stop just inside the covered area. He could not be seen from outside. Luigi smiled, gasped for air, and heaved a deep sigh of relief as he got comfortable in the position he might be stuck in for quite a while. Cool water continually washed down the slide, cascading around his body and over his head, bringing freshness and relief. He relished his victory. *God, I swear I'll spend my life doing good and I'll lose fifty pounds if you get me out of this.*

He spent a moment mourning the loss of his friend and lover and wishing he hadn't stopped to play that piano today. Luigi had no idea that the blood from his wounds trickled into the stream of clean water making its way down the slide and cascading into the wading pool below. Nadina

Hanad stood by the pool and grinned at blood circling and

swirling, turning the water pink. The deadly Amazon

pivoted forty-five degrees, raised her weapon, and sighted

the exact center of the opaque section of plastic between her

and her quarry. Wasting not another second, she tore apart

the slide with a hail of gunfire. The plastic separated as

though machine-perforated. Luigi's body hung suspended

above the pool for a moment, rotated a little, and fell with a

thud and a splash, the slide collapsing around him.

CHAPTER FORTY

Doctors Menti and Sampson waited longer than the fifteen minutes they had given Nurse Desiree, then called the ship and got no answer. Repeated attempts brought the same results.

"Steve, this is serious.-Something bad is happening on that boat," Menti said. He called out to his receptionist, telling her to cancel the rest of his appointments for the day, then grabbed Steve's arm and shepherded him to Menti's private office.

"Get on the computer. Look for and call numbers to get in touch with anyone from that cruise line," he told Steve, "I'm going to see if I can call in favors and get a copter out to that ship. I'll see if I can't get a doctor flown out, too, rather than try to get Robby to a hospital. The faster we make things happen, the better."

"Thanks," Steve responded, "I really appreciate this." He began Googling for the OAR company website.

****

With Erasto and Taban gone, Nurse Desiree's hands shook as though she'd been operating a jackhammer. She grabbed one hand with the other to still the tremors and calm herself. She desperately wanted a smoke, or a drink, or a pill — anything to soothe her nerves — but that wouldn't be happening. Desiree looked into the other room and watched Jo stroke her son's hair. She turned to medical books on the shelves, found, and pulled out the one she needed. Desiree looked up *Appendectomy*, folded the page, and then carried the book into the other room.

"I'm going to perform the appendectomy on your son," Nurse Desiree, said as she arranged instruments and pulled pills out of a medical cabinet.

"No, you're not doing anything of the kind," Jo said with conviction.

"Listen to me, because you have a simple choice here." Desiree answered the objection with studied calmness and a sense of authority. "In case you didn't see the guys with the gun to my head, I'm telling you this ship is under attack. Our doctor is dead. Your son, as sure as I'm standing here, has a ruptured appendix. You can sit and wait for help to arrive, but that doesn't seem likely right now, does it?" She looked at the wire-filled hole on the wall where the phone used to be. "If that's what you want, I'll sit with you and hold your sons hand. We'll give him pain meds and pray that his insides don't get infected. In all likelihood, they will. He'll die."

Jo fought tears and hysteria. On the edge of exhaustion, she felt as though she were drowning and couldn't keep her children from going under with her.

Vaguely, she heard the nurse's voice go on, "Or you can get yourself together and help me take out his appendix, giving him a solid chance to live."

"B-but have you ever done anything like this before?"

"No, ma'am, I have not. But it's a pretty straight-forward procedure and I have assisted or watched many times," Desiree lied. She had seen it done twice, and she knew once you cut into flesh anything can happen. She leaned toward Jo and put a hand on her shoulder.

"I can do this. But I need your support and your assistance. Can you work with me?" Jo nodded. Nurse Vomit pondered just what the hell she would do next.

****

Steve Sampson quickly found the OAR website and a list of emergency phone numbers for each ship. Because they had failed to reach the *Treasure of The Seas,* he dialed headquarters' main phone number and began an eleven-minute odyssey dealing with ignoramuses and incompetents, but he eventually landed the name of the company's Chief Security Officer. Unfortunately, the man's answering machine stated that he was out of the office, and Steve began the whole cluster fuck a second time to get someone to page the guy.

Meanwhile, Dr. Menti managed to get in touch with the operations director at Roy Lester Schneider Hospital on St. Thomas Island. George Crandall immediately recognized the seriousness in Menti's voice and understood the potential gravity of the situation, if the story were true. While they talked, Crandall Googled Dr. Menti and found that there was such a surgeon.

"Do you mind if I dial you right back, Doctor?" Crandall asked. He feared being the victim of a prank. Menti, exasperated, agreed and hung up. Two minutes later, Crandall was on the line with him again.

"Can you put a surgeon on a chopper and get him out to that ship? And how fast, Mr. Crandall?" Menti wanted to know.

"Well, sir, I want to help, but it's not that easy," responded Crandall, rubbing his almost hairless scalp. "Usually we're notified by the ship's crew about a medical emergency."

"I understand that," replied Menti, "We're trying to contact the ship, but it seems all communication is shut down."

"And I understand that, Doctor. As we're speaking, I've sent an assistant to get our emergency physician to standby, and I've called our pilot via his beeper. But the helicopter doesn't fly free, and we must have approval from the cruise line before we send it out. No exceptions."

Dr. Menti paused for a moment, digesting, and then understood fully what he meant. "Mr. Crandall, what can I do to assure you that the helicopter will be paid for in full?"

"Doctor, can I put you on hold while I speak with my superior?" was the controlled response from Crandall.

Meanwhile Steve had managed to get a page sent out for OAR's Chief Security Officer, Jonathon Breslow. Breslow was in a meeting and was none too happy when his secretary pulled him out to talk to the frantic father of a passenger.

"Mr. Breslow, I understand you're a busy man. My name is Dr. Steve Sampson. My wife, daughter, and son are currently on one of your cruise ships, the *Treasure of The Seas*, and they are in the middle of a medical emergency."

Breslow interrupted, "Sir, I believe they've put you through to the wrong office. I'm Chief of Security, not medical. I'll see that you're transferred to the correct office."

"Don't you dare *transfer* me!" Steve shouted into the phone. "My son could die if you do not authorize a helicopter to get to that ship. The communications are down out there. Can you at least try to contact the ship while I wait on the line? Please, humor me and do that for me, sir!"

Breslow pulled the phone away from his face, covered the mouthpiece, and motioned his secretary into the room.

"Mr. Sampson, I'm going to put you on hold for a moment. Is that alright?"

"Sure, whatever, but hurry," Steve answered.

"Is James in the building today?" Breslow asked his secretary, referring to Billington III.

"Yes," she said. "Shall I get him?"

"Not yet." He dialed the ship's emergency number, to no avail. Then he called the bridge, the Captain's cell phone, Chief Security Officer, the navigational office, the Purser's

office, and the Cruise Director's office. No answers
anywhere.

"Get James and anyone else in upper management
here quickly, immediately," he told his secretary as he
clicked the hold button back to Steve Sampson.

"Mr. Sampson, no need to panic. We seem to have a
communication satellite malfunctioning. I assure you; we're
working on it from our end and will have it back up as soon
as possible."

"With all due respect, sir, I don't give a rat's ass about
your communications problem," said Steve. "Just authorize
the damn helicopter!"

"Steve," Dr. Menti cut in, "I've got a chopper. It's
leaving now with a doctor on board."

"I don't know if you heard that, Breslow, but we just
authorized our own damned helicopter. I suggest you guys

get your heads out of your asses and find out what's going

on out there aboard your own ship!"

Breslow lowered the phone as James Billington III,

Chief Executive Officer Reid Klein, and Chief Financial

Officer Fen Jacobs walked into the room.

"What seems to be the problem?" Billington asked

Breslow.

"I'm not sure. I've got a ship dead in the water and no

way to communicate with her."

"Outrageous," said Billington. "So your satellite is

down. Just e-mail somebody."

Breslow rolled his eyes, but Billington missed the

gesture. If the satellite was indeed out, e-mail would be

down as well, but no one knew yet what the true issue was.

Point of fact: No one on the *Treasure* responded to any kind

of query. Breslow bounced his fist off the desk and his eyes

lit up. He nodded to himself and said out loud, "I've got an idea. That ship should be at OAR Cay today — give me a second here." He dialed the OAR Cay medical facility and breathed a huge sigh of relief when a human actually answered his call.

"Get me the highest ranking ship official on that island right now," he yelled.

"Certainly," came a meek response, "Who may I say is calling?"

"This is OAR Chief Security Officer Jonathon Breslow — now move it or you're fired!"

In moments, Breslow heard a voice come across, "Hello, this is Chief Petty Officer Ingmar Swenson. To whom am I speaking?"

"OAR Chief Security Officer, Jonathon Breslow. When was the last time you, or any other employee, were in contact with the *Treasure*?"

"Well, sir, that's just the thing. The shuttles between the island and the ship stopped running and we can't contact the ship to find out what's going on. I'm told that earlier, a few passengers reported hearing sounds like gunfire from the direction of the ship."

"Gunfire?" Breslow barked.

"They described kind of a rat-a-tat, like fire crackers, you know. It was brief and a one-time thing, nothing serious, I believe. Probably an engine backfiring. Everything is fine here on the Cay."

"You idiot! Why did no one call security when they heard gunfire?" Breslow, beginning to boil, realized he was getting angry with the wrong man, and he had no trouble understanding that things could be a lot worse out there than he'd originally thought. "Let me talk to your security supervisor."

Taking in that conversation, Billington closed Breslow's office door and the three waiting executives sat down on the couch and chairs. Billington tapped his foot rapidly. Reid Klein ran a finger around the band of his collar like a cartoon cliché, and Fen Jacobs cracked his knuckles one at a time.

Swenson's voice came back with a tremor, "Sir, there doesn't seem to be any security personnel on the island at this time. Can I get someone else for you?"

"Listen up, Swenson. You are hereby deputized by me. You are acting on my behalf. Do you have a cell phone?"

"Yes sir, however…"

"Don't interrupt again, we don't have time. Leave the medical office and head to the back part of the island. Find the cove with a covered area — you know, the one where maintenance is performed. There's a small motor boat stored there. Get in it — get out to the ship, and find out what's going on. Move it!"

Swenson gave Breslow his cell number, too intimidated to reveal that he had no idea how to start a motor boat. He had never even been in one.

Confident that he had the ball rolling; Breslow hung up and dialed his secretary. "I want every head of security on every one of our ships at sea to phone in here immediately. I'm declaring code red right now." He turned to Billington. "Code red okay with you, sir?

Billington had no idea. *What the hell was code red?* "What do you think the problem is, Jonathon?" he asked, hedging. His foot tapping accelerated.

"I believe our fleet is under a nine-eleven-type terrorist attack. Code red returns all ships to their home ports as soon as they account for passengers and crew. We'll alert the U.S. Coast Guard and the authorities of all countries and territories we have ships in."

Billington stopped tapping. Unbelievably, he had only one question. "What's this going to cost?"

CHAPTER FORTY-ONE

Dalmar walked onto the Captain's bridge, fully

realizing he was about to make his prowess and greatness

public. He would contact OAR cruise lines — they'd be

shocked to hear two things. One, he had control of their

ship, and, two, they must pay handsomely if they desired its

safe return. His head swelled a little more. He had pulled off

the taking of this vessel with relative ease. *Why hadn't he*

thought of this before? The security was quite a bit easier to get

around than he'd thought. In fact, he probably could have

boarded by force without having the head of security in his

back pocket. Cruise ship security was half-hearted, at best.

There were bells and whistles to assuage passengers'

nervousness, but that stuff was ineffective against his well-

conceived takeover. Dalmar made a mental note about loose

security for next time, although perhaps this success would

tighten security on cruise ships. *No worries, I'll bring more crew.* He preened in the thought that he was about to become the most famous pirate of all time. Others would stand in line to join him on future missions.

"Dial OAR's emergency number for Amina," he ordered Doratai. Then he told Amina, "Let them know that their cruise liner, the *Treasure of the Seas,* has been commandeered and our demands will follow. Tell them only what I went over with you yesterday, no other details. Understand?"

Doratai complied, identified Breslow at the other end of the call, and handed the phone to Amina.

"To whom am I speaking?" asked Amina.

"This is OAR Chief Security Officer, Jonathon Breslow. And you are?"

Amina ignored his question. "Mr. Jonathon Breslow, your ship, the *Treasure of the Seas,* has been boarded and is under the control of Abdi Dalmar."

Dalmar smiled, nodding and inflating his chest while Amina continued as she had rehearsed.

"The crew and passengers are our hostages and we will give you our demands shortly. This is between us and OAR, no one else. Do not get the United States authorities or any other government authorities involved. We will deal with you only. Make sure, Mr. Breslow, that we speak with you, personally, the next time we call."

Breslow couldn't think of anything to say. The line went dead. He bowed his head and moved it side-to-side, the gesture speaking volumes.

"What is it? Jonathon, what's going on?" Billington demanded.

"Sir, the *Treasure of the Seas* is hijacked and taken over by terrorists."

Billington stood up, stunned. "Who's captain of that ship?" he asked. "What did the terrorists say they want?" He swiped a clammy hand over his even clammier forehead, squeezing his eyes shut and biting his lip. "This could destroy our whole company — the whole cruising industry. What the hell should we do?"

Breslow watched the executive for a moment, fully realizing he would get no support or help from this man. He knit his brows, his thoughts racing.

"The captain is Gunnar Fredrickson, a good man — that is, if he's still alive. They said they'll call back with demands. Our first priority is the wellbeing of our passengers and crew."

"No, Mr. Breslow," Billington countered, "I don't mean to sound like a cliché, but our first priority is damage control. Without that, we may never have future passengers. Somebody get Avery Jentelle in here and let's make sure that when the press gets wind of this, they get it correctly — the way *we* wish them to hear it."

While public relations took center stage at OAR, Captain Gunnar, working his way to the Aqua Lounge, scanned faces, aware of his low-grade fear that someone might recognize him and give him away. He grabbed a black baseball cap off a chair and pulled it low over his eyes. There were maybe a few hundred passengers in the lounge. He watched Korfa Osman walk to the back door, and he saw Nadafi Tenge at the head of the room. Tenge stood in front of three large doors with a cursive *T,* for *Treasure,* etched into the glass of each.

Korfa stood, holding the manifest of passengers still aboard, but he had no intention of cross-checking it to figure out who was missing. He had decided that missing passengers in cabins or stowed away somewhere else posed no threat anymore. Korfa padlocked the back door and headed for the front, while Nadafi padlocked two of the three entrance doors. As passengers noticed the two strangers locking doors, a tense nervousness overtook the room.

Korfa, having reached Nadafi, turned and addressed the group. "Ladies and gentlemen, I shall ask to you please stay calm. We do not intend to hurt you if you follow instructions. Find yourself a seat and stay in it. My friend here likes to shoot and ask questions later, so don't upset him. Hopefully, this will be over quickly and you can go back to your cruise vacation."

"What's this all about?" yelled a senior citizen sitting in a motorized wheelchair. "You can't hold us here against our will!" He pushed a joy stick to propel his chair toward the front door, but Nadafi came down to meet him and blocked the chair with his body. He leaned in to the wheelchair occupant and spoke.

"Sir, I am assuming you were once a soldier for your country?"

The man looked confused, and then answered, "United States Marine Corps. Served two tours in Korea."

"I knew that about you," said Nadafi, smiling. "I could tell you are a warrior by the way you carry yourself. I too, am a warrior for my country, and sir, I believe I hold the floor, so to speak, do I not?" He leaned in closer and whispered, "Sir, you are trained to offer resistance, but let me arm you with as much information as possible. If you continue further opposition, you are placing not only yourself but the rest of these fine people in jeopardy. We are heavily armed and have a job to do. When we are finished we will leave you unharmed, but if you fail to stand down I will not be able to help you. Now, I have recognized your leadership skills. I hope you recognize mine and implore your fellow passengers to relax while we do our jobs. Are we in agreement?"

The man nodded and backed up. He wedged his chair between two isle seats and turned the key to *off*. He sat still as if to gather his thoughts, Nadafi figured, maybe deciding to address the crowd. Then the Marine got out of the chair and took a step toward Nadafi, saying, ""I am a United States Marine. My rank is corporal. My name is Bill...."

Nadafi gave up. He shot the man between the eyes and watched him fall back into his chair. "I have no interest in your name or your rank or serial number, nor in playing any other games," he told the body laying half on the chair and half on the floor. Nadafi raised his head and addressed the crowd again. "Please," he said, sighing in exasperation. He held his hands apart, arms extended as if supplicating. "No more fools. We do not wish to harm you. But you can see we will do what we need to do to accomplish our mission. Now shut up, all of you."

The room fell silent. Smells of gunfire and fresh blood wafted through the air. Passengers retreated, scooting their chairs as far away from the doors and the two pirates as they could get, forming an uncomfortable knot of bodies in the center of the lounge. Some exchanged looks and glances, but no one spoke. One woman, searching faces with her eyes, looked directly into Captain Gunnar's eyes and stopped. She brightened, almost lurching forward as she recognized him, but Gunnar put his index finger to his lips for a quick second and begged her silence with the widening of his eyes.

CHAPTER FORTY-TWO

Jen, Cullen, and Elaine continued cautiously down the long hallway of deck nine and Elaine asked her husband, "What do we do next?"

"Well, I need to find my mom and my brother," Jen said.

"Honey, we should follow Cullen right now," Elaine countered.

"Why should we follow *him*? I don't know if I should be following anyone."

"I'll tell you why, dear, because he's a God damned expert killer and he's in his element, if you get my drift. He's like a shark that smells blood in the water. Truth is I think he actually knows what he's doing. Now let's let him do his thing and get us the hell out of here!"

Jen looked at the woman and shook her head disgustedly.

"What's your problem?" asked Elaine.

"I just don't understand how you could sleep in the same bed with him. If you know what he is, how can you stay with him?"

"We all have our own reasons for doing stupid shit, don't we, honey? I'll give you my excuses when you give me yours."

"Ladies, can we forget for a moment about what a monster I am? Jen, I promise we'll look for your mom, but we've got to get to the Aqua Lounge where they sent the other passengers. That's probably where Jo and Robby are, anyway. If there's a way we can get passengers off the ship and out of danger, we do that first."

"My hero," Elaine drawled, touching elbows with Jen. "He believes whole-heartedly in the sanctity of human life, so he wants to save as many of them as possible." Her tone dripped sarcasm, so Jen chimed in.

"Probably so he can kill them later." The two snickered.

"I'm glad you two are bonding at my expense." This from Cullen.

"Sorry, dear, but it's not like we're going to enjoy the buffet tonight, or take in a show. You're all the entertainment we've got."

They moved towards the stairway, unaware that Nadina Hanad had heard them talking and waited underneath. She grabbed Jen's foot and pulled her down the stairs. The teen tumbled head-over-heels once, then executed a perfect head-tuck forward roll as though she were back in gymnastic class. Elaine bowled herself into Nadina full force to protect Jen, but she bounced off Nadina's muscular frame like she'd hit a brick wall and crumbled, broken, to the ground. Nadina drew her knife, plunged it into Elaine's chest, and twisted it in a violent motion. Jen, screaming, pushed herself back to the wall as far as she could while

Cullen, seeing the whole thing in slow motion, pulled out

his pistol and fired into Nadina's left bicep. Nadina grabbed

the wound. Elaine sank to the ground and gulped for air, her

breath rattling. Nadina reached for her gun but Cullen put a

second round into her right bicep. The Amazon dropped to

her knees, cradling her bleeding arms, and grinned at

Cullen.

"Finish!" she screamed at him. "Do you have the

balls?"

Elaine managed one more breath and one more

thought – *Lady, they are the size of an elephant's. You don't know*

*the half of it...*and both Elaine and Nadina Hanad were gone.

CHAPTER FORTY-THREE

The OAR executives moved their base of operations from Jonathon Breslow's office to a large private conference room. Present, along with Breslow and James Billington III, were Reid Klein and Fen Jacobs — all awaited the arrival of Vice President of Public Relations Avery Jentelle. CEO Reid Klein ran OAR on a day-to-day basis. People knew him as an outgoing person with an ingratiating style that allowed him to fire a person and have them leave his office feeling like they'd been given a raise and an opportunity for advancement.

"You've got to make them feel like they aren't part of the problem, but their termination is part of an answer and will benefit the company they love," he told his secretary.

He had mostly grey hair speckled with black and a solid build that made him appear to be in his early fifties, although he was pushing sixty. Klein's perpetual smile reflected his love of the job and the people he worked with; his employees were his family, and when he shook their hands he conveyed genuine warmth to them. Of the top company executives, Reid Klein was the most well-liked. Even employees who had never met him respected his style and his policies. Klein ran OAR during its amazing turn-around and tolerated James Billington III as the figurehead raking in accolades and glory and boatloads of cash. After all, it was Billington's company, but Klein felt a certain sting being the number one guy, yet not getting credit publicly. Klein's obscene salary and multitudinous perks soothed his ruffled feathers.

If Reid Klein was the gregarious leader everybody loved, Fen Jacobs, Chief Financial Officer, was Klein's polar opposite. Each day, Jacobs wore a bow tie, and each tie seemed two sizes too small for his bulging neck. By day's end, he had a red mark where the tie had abraded his skin. An intensely quiet man, his darting eyes always seemed to be keeping a secret. Suited to his position, he was consumed almost every moment by his desire to make the most money for OAR first and for Fen Jacobs second. Inclined to focus on the paper in front of him at a given moment, he trusted real facts and figures and balked at long term plans to boost revenues *down the road*. His quiet demeanor, due to a lack of anything else to talk about besides money issues, often made him a bad guy to the rank and file. While the reputation may have been undeserved, that image was exactly what Reid Klein wanted when he'd hired his old college buddy — a yin to Klein's yang. In rough times, Klein cast Jacobs as financial fall guy, an advantage in negotiations with employees or other organizations. It went like this, "I'm sorry, if it were up to me, I'd meet your price point, but my CFO says we don't have the budget."

This ideally paired duo, along with James Billington III, formed a cabal commonly referred to around the company as the *Triumvirate.*

In the pecking order, Avery Jentelle, charismatic Vice President of Public Relations, ranked right below the Triumvirate. Her long auburn hair feathered flirtatiously to the side and she spoke with a slight wisp of the Southern accent she had acquired growing up in South Carolina. In days past, she might have been guilty of exploiting her feminine traits and wiles, but as she progressed up and up in the good-old-boy business world, she'd become more confident and now dazzled them with style, bravado, innovativeness, and brains. Blessed with many feminine assets, she chose to hide them beneath expensive, colorful suits — her "man suits" — and flaunt her long legs, uplifted breasts, and firm rear end only when needed for the job. That wasn't often, now that she had reached her mid-forties and held executive status.

Klein had hired Avery away from the corporate offices of a national hamburger chain. She set James Billington III out in front on TV advertising and national print campaigns. Her stroke of genius paid off in huge profits and enormous recognition for Billington and for OAR. It also put her smack in Billington's line of sight, establishing her credibility forever.

When things turned sour, however, Avery thrust herself front and center for media jackals, so Billington remained the good guy. When someone leaked that a ship's cleanliness rating dipped or that a virus had broken out on board another, Avery, ever the PR pro, answered questions and calmed the storm. When the press discovered ship board workers with serious criminal records, Avery stood stalwartly out front of the media, cleaning up the mess. As she swept into the conference room now, the Triumvirate relaxed collectively, certain that Avery would be the face of this crisis and that she would rescue them before sharks circled.

"Well, what's up, gentlemen?" she asked as she positioned herself at the head of the conference table. She remained standing and said, "My staff and I are on a tight deadline for the new ad campaign. I'm on my way across town in a few minutes to check on proofs."

Jonathon Breslow reached to close the door. "Cancel it," he said.

"Okaay." Avery drew the word out and surveyed their drawn, serious expressions. "Not a flawed cleanliness report, then. Did someone fall overboard? Worse? Alright, out with it and let's control damage." She lifted her chin and folded her arms across her chest.

The Triumvirate's heads swiveled in Breslow's direction, anointing him the bearer of the bad news. Breslow didn't hesitate.

"A ship has been boarded and taken over, apparently by terrorists. No reports of casualties or deaths. All we know is that the head guy is called Abdi Dalmar."

"Wait. Wait, let me catch up here," Avery interjected. "What ship?"

"The *Treasure*."

"Where?"

"Docked off OAR Cay."

"How do you know the guys' name? What do they want?"

"The terrorists that called said Abdi Dalmar had boarded and taken over the ship. They'll call back soon with demands," Breslow gestured puzzlement with his hands and shrugged.

"What makes you think they're terrorists? You've used that word several times now. Did they identify themselves as terrorists?"

"No. What's the difference? Abdi Dalmar sounds pretty much like a terrorist name, doesn't it?"

"Actually, to me, it sounds Middle Eastern, but it might be African," Avery spoke thoughtfully, but her mind ran ahead, contemplating possible strategies.

"Who the hell cares where the asshole is from? He's got our ship!" Breslow slumped back down and drummed his fingers.

"I'm not trying to upset you, Jonathon, but it's important to have all the facts. If it's a terrorist group looking for political headlines, we deal with it one way. If it's something else, we may approach it differently."

"They ordered us not to notify governments or Coast Guards of any sort," Reid threw in. Billington grimaced, obviously displeased at being ordered to do anything.

"Well, there you go. If they are terrorists, they would certainly want governments and everyone else to know what they're doing" Avery said, satisfied that she'd impressed them.

"What are you thinking?" Billington cut to the chase.

"Hmm, I'm thinking if it's a terrorist thing, we've got a long drawn-out event on our hands; but if it's somebody who wants a ransom, we'll act quickly to minimize damages and protect passengers. Do we know if anyone of great wealth is aboard, a target?"

"What funds do we have available to offer, Fen?" Reid queried in an aside to the CFO.

"Wait a second," Breslow waved a hand and leaned forward, glaring at the two men. "If one single rich guy is the target, then somebody else should pay up. You guys are talking offers before you even get a demand?"

"It doesn't hurt to be prepared," Reid answered and looked toward Fen for input.

"I guess I'll check petty cash," Fen joked, clearly on Breslow's side.

The joke fell flat and the room went meaningfully silent for a few seconds before Reid resumed.

"Do we agree, then?" he paused and jerked his head at the phone. "We're not calling for government help?" They each nodded in turn, although Fen, the last, appeared reluctant.

"Moving on. I'll tell ya'll it wouldn't hurt a bit if we knew something about this Dalmar guy before we have to talk to him," Avery said, nodding to Breslow.

"I've got a guy who can help us," he responded, but the phone's ring ended his thought.

CHAPTER FORTY-FOUR

With tightness in her stomach and a lump in her throat nurse Desiree sedated Robby. While the medication kicked in, she prepped and sanitized the area where she would cut into the child's skin. Tears welled in Jo's eyes as she looked at her son. She thought of him running around the house, knocking over plants and pictures, spilling his third cup of milk at dinner and innocently claiming it wasn't his fault. *Right now,* she thought, *he looks like his most innocent and helpless self.*

Jo breathed deeply through her surgical mask and picked at the light green surgical gown Nurse Desiree had given her. Again, she went over the positives and negatives of what they were about to do. She understood that if nothing were done he would get sicker and probably die. She understood how unlikely it would be that this nurse could do everything right as she cut open Jo's only son. But really, what was the choice? *I was dealt these cards, and I have to play them.* She steeled herself, calling on everything she had learned in her career of covering heart-breaking news stories. Jo's eyes followed the blade as Nurse Desiree slid a scalpel lightly across Robby's abdomen once, almost like a golfer practicing her swing, then pressured the blade into his skin hard enough to make the incision. The first trickle of blood formed under the silver knife.

****

Dr. Menti ended his conversation with George Crandall. He felt satisfied that a chopper, with an emergency room surgeon strapped in behind the pilot, made its way towards the *Treasure of the Seas.* At first, Menti beamed with a sense of accomplishment, reveling in his power to cut through red tape and get the job done. He'd actually offered a twenty-five thousand dollar bribe on top of whatever other costs might be incurred by the hospital, figuring he'd deal later with whether or not he would actually pay that sum. To Crandall's and the hospital's credit, they turned down the bribe and dispatched the helicopter. They did, however, mention that a donation to help with construction of their planned kidney facility would be greatly appreciated. Dr. Menti loved the sound of the *Dr. Michael Menti Kidney Center* at Roy Lester Schneider Hospital.

Steve Sampson's luck fell somewhat below Menti's. Steve called OAR seeking more details and hoping to mend fences with Jonathon Breslow. The OAR switchboard was shut down and all calls went directly to general voice mail. Frustrated, he thought briefly about calling the television station his now ex-wife worked for. If anything could launch butts into gear, it would be a call from media, especially TV media. Dispelling that impulse, he chose to text Jennifer again.

Jen - am trying to contact ship's hospital to help with Robby. Can't get through! What is going on?

Jen jumped when her phone shrilled the arrival of a text, and, reading the message, she set the phone to vibrate. Her survival might depend on details. Now, what should she reply to her dad?

Yeah, Dad, ship overtaken by terrorists and I'm trying to rescue passengers. By the way, my partner is a crazy murderer that I witnessed killing somebody. I just watched his wife get stabbed right in front of me and saw him kill a few more people. Don't panic. Love you.

Deciding against the whole truth, she typed:

I'm safe. The ship is under attack! I haven't seen mom or Robby but am trying to get to them. Call the Coast Guard or something. I know this sounds crazy - but I'm serious!

Steve stood up while he read and crossed the room to show Menti the message. Dr. Menti looked at Steve and sank into the chair. "I'll call the Coast Guard. I don't know why I didn't do that in the first place."

"I'm calling the television station," Steve said, in the process of dialing.

****

Ingmar Swenson found the small boat in the lagoon. He pulled a green, moldy tarp off the top and gingerly stepped inside the craft. It must have been used recently, since quite a bit of water pooled in the bottom. Two orange life vests with the OAR logo on them soaked in the puddle and he put on the less soaked of the two before turning toward the motor. *Ok, I have to start this.* He remembered starting a tractor at home — you put the engine in choke and give the chord a few pulls to prime the motor. He did that and congratulated his effort. *Now, put it into start and hope for the best.* Mentally, Swenson high-fived himself when the engine started after three pulls. He eased the boat forward, bumping the dock once or twice, and then guided it out of the lagoon and around the back of the island to head for the *Treasure of the Seas*. He hadn't a clue what or who he should look for and cursed his luck for being closest to the phone when Breslow had called.

The fifteen minutes it took him to navigate to the ship were probably the most stressful of his life. One moment he thought, *Cool, I can do this.* In the next, he feared for his life, marveling at how he could possibly have gotten to this life-and-death situation. He'd only signed on to enjoy working in the sun and sand for a festive cruise ship.

Ingmar, in the spreading shadows of Treasure's massive bow, could see two shuttle boats clinging to the right side of the ship. Squinting, he picked out one man in each shuttle and decided to get closer before he called Breslow. For several more minutes he maneuvered through choppy waves, hoping to get close enough to hail the men.

He decided to keep a safe distance in case he had to turn and make a run for it, though he worried that his small motor boat might not outrun the shuttles.

Ani Azar and Chill watched Ingmar's approach from their respective boats. Each silently debated calling Dalmar, but each chose not to. One man. Tiny boat. Little threat.

"Is everything all right out here?" Ingmar called. "I say, do you need help of any kind?" Ani did not speak, but he waved his hands in the air motioning Ingmar back to the island. Ingmar pressed the issue.

"Why aren't you shuttling back to the island? Is there something wrong with your boats?"

Ani, still mute, continued to wave Ingmar off, but the OAR employee, pleased with his accomplishment so far, wasn't having any. "I have been ordered by the head of OAR security to find out if I can be of assistance!"

Something in the water caught the corner of Ingmar's eye and he glanced over, then craned his head far to the left. Dumbfounded, he watched several human heads bob up and down in the surf. Terror walked up Ingmar's spine and he acted, he hoped, as though he had seen nothing. Very slowly, he reversed the tiny boat that was now destined to be his salvation.

"I'll tell them everything is alright then, eh?" he called. Tasting the metallic sting of adrenaline on his tongue, he coolly turned the boat, ready to slam the accelerator to the floor. Chill moved faster, gunning his boat. He set upon Ingmar in a matter of seconds, chuckling as he realized the single-man craft had stalled when the fool aboard tried to gun it. Ingmar's motor boat lay dead in the water as Chill pulled up beside him.

"I will go back. I will say I saw nothing," cried Ingmar. "Please, I will go back!"

Chill stared into Ingmar's wide-open, glassy eyes. "I am in the same position as you, sir. We're both in the wrong place at the wrong time. I'm very sorry."

Ingmar turned and ducked. Chill's three bullets thumped into the OAR hero's back.

CHAPTER FORTY-FIVE

I'd like to talk to Russ Donovan, please," Steve told

the operator for WTAM Television, Tampa.

Donovan, news director for the station that employed

Jo, was a hulking man with a beer belly he displayed

proudly and unselfconsciously. Direct and forward thinking,

he led his newsroom dynamically, commanding respect and

top-quality work. Though he looked imposing, he loved his

staff and crew and despised the suits that ran the station. He

never let the suits' idea of making a dollar interfere with his

journalist's view of the world, but he understood the fine

line he walked between the station's need to turn a profit

and the news operation's desire to report accurately. This

political skill worked best for him when he stood in the

middle and caused all parties to play nicely together.

Russ came on the line and Steve snapped his attention to the call. "Russ, Steve Sampson here. Look, I've got something rather important I'd like to run by you."

Donovan creaked back in his oversized leather chair and patted his impressive gut. "Sure, Steve — what's up? We've got to do that golf thing we talked about." He rocked, stroking his signature Fu Manchu mustache and deciding it could use a waxing. He twirled the distinctive attribute between his thumb, index, middle, and right ring fingers as he talked.

Steve blurted, "My wife and kids are on a cruise ship and some strange things are going on."

"Yeah, I knew Joanne was on vacation this week. And hey, buddy, I'm sorry to hear about you two. Real shame."

At work Russ was singularly focused and intense, yet pleasant to be around. When he got away from work he was singularly focused and intense about having a good time.

His Irish blood loved to party. When the six o'clock news
ended on Friday nights, he rambled out the door to have a
blast at whatever pub called to him that week.

It was at these Friday night shindigs that Steve got to
know and grow fond of the big fellow. They'd chatted often
about politics and the news business. They discovered a
mutual love for the Tampa Bay Buccaneers and the
University of Florida Gators. They were both alums.
Donovan respected Jo enormously and secretly wished she'd
consider getting back into his news room instead of working
in the suits' side of the building.

"Yeah, thanks," responded Steve, having failed to
dispense with small talk. He tried again, "Our son, Robby
had a serious attack of something — we think appendicitis
— while on board the cruise ship. While I was trying to get
help for him, all communication to or from the ship was cut
off."

Donovan prepared to dismiss Steve the same way he dealt with other people a thousand times a day. Everyone had a killer news story that really wasn't a news story.

"Okay, Steve, I'll pass the info along to our assignment editors and have someone make some calls, see what they can find out for ya, buddy. Glad you called. Okay?" He sat upright, gave the cookie duster a last twist, and took the phone off his shoulder, ready to disconnect.

"No! Wait, Dan. That's not all. I've gotten some texts from my daughter, Jennifer, indicating that the ship was taken over by armed thugs. We're thinking terrorists."

Donovan leaned forward further in his chair and started pounding his keyboard.

"You got my attention. Where are they? What ship?"

"Docked at an island owned by the cruise line. OAR Cay. They're aboard the *Treasure of the Seas.*"

"You say the line is OAR, correct Steve?" asked Donovan as he typed on his computer and twiddled his mustache. He couldn't find a news story or release about the ship, but he had a phone number on hand that might turn up some answers. He wondered about conflict of interest, but flicked the thought away, deciding it would be okay if he delegated the calls.

"Listen, buddy, you sit tight. I'm gonna have somebody make a few calls. Call you back as soon as I have anything." By the time he hung up the phone, Donovan's hand waved one of his producers into his office. He gave her a quick synopsis and sent her on her way to dig up whatever she could. He called his secretary and told her to put his anchors, Ted and Brenda, on alert for breaking news. He certainly wasn't prepared to break in with a special bulletin yet, but he'd be ready, just in case.

Some while later his producer returned, lifting her hands in defeat. "I'm not getting anywhere, can't confirm a thing, boss."

"Keep trying. Call the Coast Guard if you have to." Donovan dialed Steve's number.

"Hey, buddy, this is Donovan. We haven't been able to confirm anything yet. Let me ask you in all seriousness, Jennifer isn't prone to pranks or anything, is she? I mean, I don't want to piss you off, but I don't want to make all these calls and find out your kid was playing a practical joke. You understand, right?"

"Yes, I understand," Steve answered. "Jen's absolutely not that kind of person. She wouldn't do something like that."

"Okay." Donovan paused a moment to think, hands busy at his facial growth. "How fast can you get to the station?"

"I'm about fifteen minutes away, why?"

"Just get over here as fast as you can, okay? Oh, and

Steve — don't forget your phone."

CHAPTER FORTY-SIX

"I speak for Abdi Dalmar," Amina's golden voice came authoritatively across the phone connection. "To whom am I speaking?"

"This is Jonathon Breslow — the person you spoke to earlier — as you requested."

"Good. At least we know you can follow instructions. Here is what we expect from OAR, sir." Amina paused for dramatic effect as those in the conference room waited.

"For the safe return of your vessel, we shall expect payment of fifty million American dollars. We require a helicopter to safely transport our crew — we require the assurance of safe passage back to our home. You can see those are the simplest of demands. We know that the owner of your company is among the wealthiest men in the world and what we are asking is a pittance to him. We could easily demand more. If you do not have the money in our possession, and the helicopter on the ship, within the next three hours, we will begin destroying your ship. That will cost you a whole lot more than fifty million dollars to repair. We are rigging the ship with explosive devices set to go off in exactly three hours and thirty-one minutes, unless we override them. That allows thirty minutes beyond your deadline for our experts to disable the devices remotely after we are safely away. Do you understand and accept our demands?"

Those in the room turned to Billington, who turned to Fen Jacobs, who nodded agreement.

"We are gathering the money as we speak," answered Breslow. "You must assure us that passengers and crew will be unharmed."

Amina snapped back, "Mr. Breslow. You are not in control here. I see you're new to this game, so let me explain how it works. We make demands. You meet those demands. Simple. Am I clear?"

Breslow was embarrassed but forged on, "Can I ask what group you represent?"

"We represent ourselves! Now, we will call back in one hour, and we will need a progress report from you. Goodbye, Mr. Breslow."

A curtain of immobilized silence hung over the room. After reestablishing her poise, Avery Jentelle spoke. "They're not terrorists, Jonathon." He glared at her with hateful eyes.

"How the hell do you know? You deal with damage control, and I'll deal with whatever these people are."

Avery stood up and folded her arms, not intimidated. "They're not terrorists."

"Then what the hell are they, madam expert?"

"They're holding the *ship* hostage, correct? Not the *passengers*! Terrorists would threaten and kill passengers. They'd make political statements. You've seen that. We all have."

"I really don't see the difference," Billington carped. "They want fifty million dollars of my money. Our only option is to hand the money over, am I correct?"

"There is a significant difference I can see," Avery said. "Organized terrorists blow stuff up first and then make demands. It's my guess that they aren't going to blow anything up, because they don't have the firepower."

"Make your point already, Avery." Reid said.

"My point is simple," she fired back. "You don't have to pay them *anything*!"

"Now that's just brilliant, Miss Public Relations Lady!" Breslow shouted. "We don't pay, they start shooting our passengers, and nobody takes a cruise for the next ten years. OAR sinks just like that ship might. Maybe you should leave the thinking to men trained to think!" Instantly, Breslow knew he'd crossed a line. He sensed the uneasiness in the room and decided he couldn't afford things to turn hostile toward him. He shut up.

Avery turned her computer around for the rest of them to see. She had found a story about Somali pirates — in every paragraph, Dalmar's name almost jumped off the screen. "Gentlemen, he's a pirate. And he's a long way from home," she said, a ghost of a smirk on her lips.

"A goddamned pirate. Why don't we prepare two satchels of money," Fen said. "One we fill with real cash and the other with Monopoly money, for all I care. Then you give them their helicopter, and after he's on his merry little way have the Air Force blow his ass out of the sky."

"Well, I wasn't prepared to go that far," added Avery. "The priority is to get them off the ship and away from the passengers. We can spend the fifty million on fixing our shitty security."

Breslow ached to hurl more abuse at this bitch but held his tongue.

"All right, let's calm down," Reid said. "I don't have to ask you, Fen, because I know you're on board with not giving up fifty million." He turned to Billington. "It's really your company and your money, James. What do you want to do?"

Billington dragged his hands through his hair and sighed. He looked at Avery. He glanced around the table. He took a sip of cold coffee. "What I'm worried about, Avery, is if this backfires and the media crucifies us, we'll drop fifty million a month in fighting bad publicity. Look, a payoff isn't going to affect the way *I* live. In case you haven't read a magazine lately, I'm doing pretty well. It's you and the rest of the employees that will be in trouble."

He paced the room and then spoke again without meeting anyone's eyes.

"That being said, I trust Avery's instincts. I think she's right — they're bluffing." He turned to Breslow. "I *know* she's right that our security is shitty, and when this is all over, I guarantee you a full investigation into how pirates overpowered your people and commandeered a half-a-billion dollar cruise ship. Here's my call — get a helicopter out there and make them think they have fifty million dollars. Let's get this over with."

As if to punctuate the stress and drama palpable in the room, someone began pounding frantically on the door. Avery's secretary burst into the room, freaked out and on the edge of tearing her hair. Gesturing like an Italian orator, she ranted, "Avery, I tried not to disturb you, but I have that incredibly aggressive television journalist calling for you. He will not go away. He wants a comment — something about

one of our ships being taken over by terrorists."

How the hell is that possible Jonathon thought, leveling

a keen glance at Avery. We've just found it out ourselves.

CHAPTER FORTY-SEVEN

Once the shock of a killing had dulled, the passengers scattered themselves around the Aqua Lounge and talked quietly in small groups. Captain Gunnar wondered where it all got away from him. It went without saying that this was the worst cruise of his career. First, he'd almost let himself romance a passenger. Then some kid passenger is accused of stealing and she accuses another of murder. His ship had been taken over by terrorists, who apparently had killed most of his crew and several passengers. If they found out his rank, surely he would be the next to die. His mind called for action, but his limbs atrophied at the thought. Every time he considered making a move, his arms and legs became stacks of marshmallows. One step would collapse him. He would definitely *not* be up for OAR Captain of the Year any time soon.

An older female passenger approached Gunnar and put her face right near his ear, as though offering a social air kiss. She whispered, "I know who you are. I was at the Captain's cocktail party."

Captain Gunnar listened, constantly moving his eyes from terrorist to terrorist. The woman continued, "When are you going to put your plan into action?" He looked at her, confused, and she went on, "I can tell you've been standing here by yourself working something out. Will you let us know if we can be of help when you decide to take action?"

Is this where I am? Gunnar thought, *an old woman mocking me?*

"Listen," she said. "Sometimes it takes a special moment to grab hold of something that's been inside you all along. Sometimes the body needs to be nudged into the direction the mind wants to go." She touched his arm, "I'm just a little old lady, but I know one thing…"

"What's that?"

Her eyes, like his, circled the room taking in other passengers, "Take a look around. If I'm going to have half a chance of leaving this ship, and I don't mean in the condition that that guy is in," she nodded to the body covered by somebody's wind breaker, "you're my only chance."

Gunnar followed her train of thought and suddenly saw, with clarity, silver hair, wrinkles, and canes. He looked in the woman's eyes. Her irises were the same deep green color as Sophia Caltimano's. Eyes like the ones he'd fallen in love with so many years ago. Sylvia had had the same wisdom and the same desire for him to live up to his potential. He felt as though he could make himself do what he needed to do; Captaincy aside, a group of human beings relied on him to get them through this mess.

"Thank you," he said patting the old woman's shoulder, "I can use your help."

"Certainly, my Captain," she replied, standing as straight as she could.

"'I'm going to distract our captors, and when I do, I'd like you to go behind the curtain on the left side of the stage. You'll find a large white box on the wall — the box is labeled, *Stage Controls*."

She nodded, "Go on."

"In the box is a lever that opens the stage. It's where the performers rise up or disappear during shows. You've seen that."

"I got ya, Captain."

"Pull the lever to open the door and then get everybody down through that opening. When you get below, head to your right and you'll find the exit that gets you out of the theater. At that point I won't be able to help you — you'll be on your own."

"I can do it," she held up her folded arthritic hands. "You can count on me."

"One more thing, once you get below locate the grey wall box with a large red handle. Once the stage closes behind you, pull that handle to pop the breaker so you can't be followed. There's no way they can open that stage trap then."

"But how will you get out?" He said nothing and she looked at him for a long moment. "Well, my good Captain, how about that! Am I to surmise that you are prepared to, as they say, go down with your ship? You might be underestimating yourself."

"Just be ready when I approach them," he answered with a slight smile. If he were to follow those passengers, he'd likely have to kill one, or maybe both of the terrorists. After long contemplation, he felt unsure that he could. He would fight as hard as he was able, but he was a cruise ship captain, not commander of a Navy destroyer. He knew he

could shoot, but he had little faith in his ability to shoot to

kill.

CHAPTER FORTY-EIGHT

Cullen and Jen reached the outside doors of the Aqua
Lounge, and, peering inside, could see one of the terrorists
through the glass. Jen's phone vibrated another message
from her father.

*Need you to be straightforward and tell us everything
going on. I am at mom's TV station and we are trying to get help.
Answer ASAP.* Steve waited with Russ Donovan and the two
news anchors for Jen's reply. The producer waited on
another phone for Avery Jentelle.

*The ship has been taken over by terrorists. I am with one
other passenger. We killed three terrorists. Trying to figure out
how to rescue a large group of passengers held in a theatre.*

Russ Donovan read the message, tugged his
mustache, and faced his anchors.

"Jesus, they're about to stage a rescue attempt. You
two get to the studio. Let everyone know we have breaking

news, and we'll be breaking into programming as soon as

we get some kind of confirmation. Alert the graphics

department — we'll need a super-typist to transcribe texts as

they come in. Steve, I need you in the studio with your

phone."

"What for? Why me?"

"Because you're going on the air live, buddy. We

have the father of a passenger who's in the middle of a

terrorist attack on a cruise ship owned by a local company.

We're smack dab in the middle of it. This is huge and I need

you on the set, communicating with your daughter. Why

else did you bring this to me?"

"Are you sure you want to do that, Russ?" Veteran

anchorwoman Brenda wanted to know, as she fiddled with

her earpiece. "What if something goes wrong? Like, God

forbid, someone is killed? Do we really want Steve on the

set?" Almost as soon as she said it, she wished she hadn't, it was a remark a rookie might make. But she had nailed the million dollar question that Russ considered earlier, but decided not to address. As a seasoned pro, he knew how awful it would be if something went wrong. Interviewing a grieving father at the moment of his daughter's demise would be tough to watch, tough to do. He also realized he'd have a keg of highly emotional, can't-shut-the-television-off moments. He could live with that.

"That's why we pay you the big bucks — to facilitate and do the right things at appropriate moments," he answered her.

Meanwhile, the producer on terminal hold with OAR got lucky. She popped the speaker-phone button, shot up, and waved Donovan over to speak to Avery Jentelle.

"Hello, this is Avery Jentelle. What can I do for you?"

Donovan leaned over the phone. "Miss Jentelle, Russ Donovan, News Director of WTAM Television. Confirm for me that one of your cruise ships, the um, *Treasure of the Seas,* has been boarded by terrorists?"

Avery always let her adversary sweat before she dropped information or responded to queries. Now she collected herself before she spoke, sounding unruffled. "Good afternoon, Mr. Donovan. Nice to hear from you, as always. I'm not sure where you got your information, but..."

Donovan cut her off, "Come on, Avery. We're both busy people. We can play games or cut to the chase. I've confirmed that there are hostages and that at least three terrorists have been killed by passengers. Pretty lame vacation, if you've got to kill somebody to survive it. You've got tons of damage control on your hands, right? I figure I can go on the air with or without your confirmation, but I'd rather have you forthrightly confirming the correct information. Wouldn't that just look so much better, Avery?"

Avery rubbed her temples, feeling a migraine lurking way behind her eyeballs. She could not believe her ears. However, Avery was pragmatic and never hedged her bets, especially when she would clearly come up short later. She, too, understood the media game.

"Ok, Donovan. Let's talk reality. I'll confirm an attempted boarding of the *Treasure of the Seas.* No formal confirmation of, or comment on, any hostages or deaths. Off the record, you need to understand that we're in sensitive negotiations and you don't want to screw that up and put people at risk, right? Then, too, you can't go on the air with any of this until families are notified. You're own reputation stands to suffer if you do, right?"

She played the TV station bad guy card to slow Donovan's advance, but he trumped her.

"Whoa, Miss Jentelle. Am I to understand that you expect me to let you notify next of kin — for over three thousand passengers — before I take a significant story live? You know me better. My dear Avery, we have a camera man in an unmarked truck, no fanfare, on his way to your office right now. I'd like you to go on the air with us and tell us yourself what you know. Please. A reporter will be with you in less than fifteen minutes." He stowed her comment about sensitive negotiations for later use, then disconnected the call and typed feverishly on his computer for a few minutes. Looking up, he waved his hand like an emperor making an edict and said to his producer, "Get your butt in gear — grab a photographer and a live truck and head to the OAR building." Not expecting further conversation, he grabbed the phone and put out a station-wide page.

"Attention!" Donovan's voice boomed through the building. He backed his mouth off the phone and began again. "All hands on deck. We are doing a live breaking news cut-in. Five minutes. All graphics and production personnel report immediately to the studio." Swiveling his chair back to the computer, he started to pound out copy.

TED:

Good afternoon, I'm Ted Stevens.

BRENDA:

And I'm Brenda Strong. We have breaking news this afternoon.

TED:

Pulse News has confirmed that a cruise ship — OAR's *Treasure of the Seas* out of Tampa — was boarded by what appear to be terrorists. We have confirmed that at least three terrorists have been killed by passengers and that possibly hundreds of passengers have been taken hostage. The ship is on a seven-day cruise out of Tampa and is currently located off OAR's private island, called OAR Cay, which is located a short distance from the Caribbean island of St. Thomas.

BRENDA:

Joining us now in the studio is Dr. Steve Sampson whose two children, as well as his ex-wife, are aboard the ship. Dr. Sampson is receiving periodic text messages from his teenage daughter, Jennifer, as events unfold. Steve, what's the last message you received?

As Steve read the message, the graphics of Jennifer's words appeared on the screen beneath a photo of Jen that Steve had provided.

Mr. Nickels and I can see the Captain and hundreds of passengers inside the Agua Lounge. There are two terrorists with machine guns — one in the front of the room the other toward the back.

Steve responded while the anchors staved off dead air with filler chat. Brenda scribbled questions for Jennifer and passed them to Steve.

Jen — who is Mr. Nickels? Where are the rest of the passengers? Have any passengers been killed or injured? Do you know who the terrorists are and what they want?

Jen, watching what she could see through the glass doors without letting herself be seen, typed replies.

Cullen Nickels. Just a heroic passenger. Most of the other passengers are off the ship on the island. Don't know if anyone has been injured or killed other than the three Mr. Nickels killed plus Mrs. Nickels, who was killed by a female terrorist. Don't know what they want. They appear to be African. OMG Captain just shot a terrorist inside the Aqua Lounge. Chaos! The passengers are running to the back of the room. Mr. Nickels is breaking through the front door to help. Passengers are escaping through opening in floor of the stage!

Ted cut in. He was as emotional as he'd ever been during his thirty years in the news business.

TED:

Folks, what you are seeing is something absolutely historic in television. You are literally living this hostage situation and seeing it via text message, as it happens. This is positively unprecedented. I have never seen anything like it, and I've been doing this for more than thirty years. And certainly we are seeing some heroic behavior. A Mr. Cullen Nickels, and the captain of the vessel, have already emerged as heroes in this ordeal. We have also learned that at least three terrorists are dead and at least one passenger has died, so far.

Brenda passed Steve another note. He typed it to Jennifer and got her reply.

Do you know where mom and Robby are?

I think down in the medical center. We were on our way there next. All the passengers have disappeared under the stage and the Captain and Mr. Nickels are gone as well. Both terrorists in the lounge are dead. Good guys five — terrorists one! I think

they forgot about me.

Jen — Robby is seriously ill. Get to him quickly. Try to

stay as close to that Mr. Nickels as you can!

Russ Donovan rushed into the control room, saying,

"Let them know we've got OAR's Vice President of Public

Relations miked up and ready to go live." The director

passed the message into Brenda's ear piece and Brenda

reacted.

BRENDA:

Joining us now is the Vice President of Public

Relations for OAR Cruise Lines, Miss Avery Jentelle. Miss

Jentelle, we have reports that at least five terrorists have

been killed and at least one passenger. Can you tell us if

anything new has developed in the past few moments?"

AVERY:

Well, no, Brenda, you seem to be ahead of us right now. We have no communication at this time with the ship. We just pray for all the passengers and hope they come out of this unharmed.

Russ Donovan spoke into Brenda's earpiece and fed her the next question.

BRENDA:

Miss Jentelle, we understand that you have been in sensitive negotiations with the terrorists. What can you tell us about their demands?

That son-of-a-bitch, thought Avery. He's damn good. You'd think he'd cut me a little slack.

CHAPTER FORTY-NINE

"I want all to check in with me right now," Dalmar shouted into his walkie-talkie. *Where are they all? What the hell is happening?*

"This is Chill," came the first response, "I had to chase down and shoot a stray officer sent from the island. Other than that, it's clear out here for me and Ani." Chill was actually very proud of himself. Kissing up to the boss didn't diminish his self-esteem one bit, and in this case he treasured anything that got him an extra few moments of life.

Dalmar waited for the next response, but the walkie-talkie was silent. "Korfa, Tenge, how are you doing with the passengers? Respond in the next five seconds!" He waited ten.

"Nadina, have you located Ghadi and Kadar? Respond in five seconds, damn it." Another ten ticked by.

He tapped a fist against his chin, scowled and looked at Amina. Pushing thumb to talk button, he barked another sentence. "We have a saboteur! Erasto, Taban, what is your location?" Again, he counted off seconds in his head, but this time he got a response in four.

"Erasto and Taban here. We are currently on deck four."

Dalmar breathed again, hardly aware that he had held his breath for such a long time. "Have you had any contact with any others?"

"Negative. We have not."

"Well, get yourselves to the Aqua Lounge and find out what happened to Korfa and Tenge."

"Yes, sir. We're two minutes out."

"Make it one!"

Jen had just sent out her last message when Erasto and Taban bounded up the stairs. She had no time to hide before they thrust their guns very near her face. *How ironic,* she thought feeling time slow to a crawl, *I really wish my serial killer was by my side.*

Without saying a word, Erasto reached out his left hand and motioned for the phone. In a flash, Jen ran through options. Throw it? Smash it? Just hand it over? She opted for the safest choice, but as she slowly lowered it to the outstretched palm; she hit the *send* button several times with her thumb. Hoping someone would get the message that she was in trouble.

Taban grabbed Jen's wrists, spun her and stuck his gun in her back. Erasto raised his arm, ready to smash the phone to smithereens.

"*Stop!*" Taban shouted. "Wait! Don't, you idiot! We need to find out who she's been talking to. Hang on to that phone." Taban grabbed his walkie-talkie and pulled out the antenna as he surveyed the damage in the Aqua Lounge.

"Dalmar, the lounge is empty. The passengers have escaped. Korfa and Tenge are both dead."

Dalmar listened, stunned. His blood boiled. He wanted to hurt something. He needed to kill something. The disembodied voice crackled again, startling him. "Sir, we have a girl. She had a phone and was in contact with somebody."

Dalmar's eyes narrowed and he pursed his lips. "Bring her to me. And bring me that phone."

Jen's heart pounded as she faced Dalmar. She wanted to run, but her legs wouldn't work. She wanted to punch, but her arms wouldn't lift. She wanted to spit, but her lips felt tight — paralyzed. Her body was exhausted. She had recently watched a man snap another man's neck, but she had no doubt that now she was looking into the face of the most evil person she'd ever set her eyes on. Dalmar looked down at her, his muscular arms folded across his chest.

Taban handed him the phone and Dalmar scrolled back and forth, reading Jen's messages. He did not lift his eyes, nor speak at all until he had gotten through the lot of them.

"You've been very busy, haven't you, young lady?" he said, slowly bobbing the phone up and down near her face. He walked around her, thinking about his next move and knowing that pacing behind her where she couldn't watch him would intimidate her.

"Gag her. Tie her to the pole," he said to Erasto. He grabbed a pager and asked Amina to flip it so every person in every corner of the ship could hear him.

"Attention, this is your captain. All passengers report back to the Aqua Lounge. Cullen Nickels — report to the bridge. Mr. Nickels, you would be wise to turn yourself in without commotion, as I will have no problem eliminating our mutual friend. I believe her name is Jen. You have three minutes to get here before I hurt her in ways I'm sure you can imagine. Also, I would like to be joined by the *former* captain of the ship, Gunnar Fredrickson."

Dalmar didn't care whether or not the passengers returned to the Aqua Lounge; he didn't have manpower to handle all those people, though they probably didn't know that yet. He did, however, very much want to meet the Captain and the mysterious Mr. Nickels. The Captain was especially valuable to him. Fredrickson and the girl might be exactly what Dalmar needed to affect an escape.

CHAPTER FIFTY

The helicopter on its way from Roy Lester Schneider

Hospital was three minutes from the *Treasure of The Seas,* and

the pilot grew frustrated with the lack of response from the

ship.

"I say again — *Treasure of the Seas.* This is medevac

chopper from St. Thomas mainland requesting permission to

land aboard the ship. We have been sent on a medical

emergency evac and we are requesting clearance to land.

Please, someone respond to our request." The pilot tried

several different frequencies, and then made sure there was

no response before he turned toward the doctor and shouted

above the roar of the chopper blades. "Well doc, it's your

call. I'm not supposed to land without a clearance, but

something doesn't feel right about this."

The medic nodded, "Let's put it down and beg

forgiveness later. This kid we're supposed to pick up has

been waiting a long time. I'd hate to turn around and leave him because someone was asleep at the wheel."

The pilot nodded back and lowered the chopper.

A flash of sunlight on the chopper blade caught Dalmar's eye and he threw the cell phone to the floor, uttering a string of curses. He watched through the giant windows surrounding the bridge, dumbfounded as the helicopter landed on the pad right outside the window, right in front of him. "What the hell do they think they're doing? Are they really trying a rescue?"

He turned toward Jen and pointed at her, spitting words now, "They're playing with your life!"

He motioned to Erasto to go out and meet the chopper. "Kill everyone aboard except the pilot. Bring him to me," Dalmar directed. Erasto headed for the door, but rethinking, Dalmar grabbed his minion's sleeve and said, "Wait. Let them land and get out, then shoot. Do not harm the pilot. We need him! Taban, you go wait for the captain and Nickels to show up. We want the Captain alive, but we don't give a shit about Nickels except to avenge our friends' deaths. Understand?"

Taban went out the door without asking any questions, but a moment later he realized he didn't know the difference between the captain and Nickels. He hoped their clothing would identify one as an officer, but he decided he'd just shoot whichever one came into view first.

As Taban walked out the door he was followed by Doratai. She could sense his indecisiveness and decided to approach.

"Taban, you have to see that everything is lost. Come with me. I can manipulate things on the computer so that we can disappear. It's our only chance."

Taban stood motionless for a moment deep in a thought about whether he would rather live or die. He looked back and could see a helicopter coming in for a landing. He decided to take his chances with Doratai.

Amina sat still, watching Jen struggle to release herself from the pole. Listening to Dalmar bark orders, she came to understand that her time with him should end. The woman realized she had clung to Dalmar for far too long. Now that Nadif was dead, she had no reason to stay with this man who was fast losing his grip. Her chances of survival were slimmer and slimmer by the minute if she stuck with him. Loyalty is well and good, but when the plan falls apart and people start dropping all over the place, it's time to fend for yourself. Decision made, she acted. Using her eyes and expressions, she tried to communicate to Jen. She faced her palms out, then down and lowered both hands toward her hips, trying to signal Jen to relax. Amina would fix this.

Nearby, but as yet undiscovered, two men set each other's fates.

"Don't you think you should loosen your grip on your little toy gun there?" Cullen asked lightly of Gunnar as they raced up the steps toward the bridge. Captain Gunnar gripped his Beretta in his white- knuckled hand. Adrenaline pulsed through him, but he realized he had to control his actions and thoughts. The gun was leading him, instead of the other way around. Gunnar slowed his pace and put his arm out to slow Cullen's as well.

"Listen, he's not going to do anything to her yet. He wants us to be there for it. We should have a plan before we give ourselves up to someone who's likely to kill us."

"Got any suggestions? I'm all ears," Cullen said. "And I don't mean to rush you, but you've got thirty seconds left to come up with this plan and I don't think you've got much experience in counter-terrorism."

Too true. Gunnar thought. He knew, suddenly, that Jen was right about Nickels. She's told the truth about seeing him kill a man, and now necessity demanded Nickels and Gunnar to bond with tough, decisive action.

"Ok," Gunnar said, "Take the gun. I'll go in first and say one of them killed you. Then you come in when, you think you've got the best chance and do...well, do whatever it is you do!" The two men took each other's measure, eye-to-eye, acknowledging a recognition of truth. Cullen was what he was, and that would save their lives, if they were lucky. They chose not to tackle this truth with words.

But Cullen spoke, "First off, Captain, I don't need the gun, but I'll take it if it makes you feel better. I like your plan. I'll be sure to tell everyone that you died a hero." Having been adversaries for three days, these two were now tossed into the same do-it-or-die bucket of crap. Dancing around issues of theft, murder, and terrorism, they agreed silently to have each other's backs for the next fifteen minutes. Straight laced, by-the-book Gunnar shook his head, and Cullen the serial killer snorted a cynical laugh, a nod to their new partnership, momentary mutual respect, and the irony of the situation they found themselves in. Then, without another word, they moved toward the bridge.

****

Directly opposite Cullen and Gunnar, outside and on the other side of the bridge enclosure, the medevac doctor jumped out of the chopper and started quickstepping toward the bridge before the blades spun down. He ran into the butt of Erasto's gun, taking a hit like a wide receiver bulldozed by a linebacker going over the middle. Erasto, training his sights on the doc, watched the man writhe in pain. The pirate was surprised when only one other person got off the helicopter and even more surprised that this pilot was a female. Erasto felt momentarily bad about shooting a doctor, but since his boss was just behind the window, watching, there was zero choice. Certain now that no one else was on the chopper, he stepped toward the pilot and motioned her hands into the air. She did. He lowered his gun and shot the struggling doctor in the stomach. The shot did not kill. The doctor screamed in disbelief and kept screaming until a second and a third bullet finished him. The pilot covered her eyes with both hands and dropped to her knees, shaking uncontrollably as Erasto walked behind her and grabbed her hair. Dalmar bolted out of the bridge door and loped across the deck toward the chopper. Nano seconds later, Captain Gunnar walked onto his own bridge with his hands raised high in the air, surrendering.

CHAPTER FIFTY-ONE

TED:

We're sorry. It appears we have lost our feed from Jennifer Sampson's cell phone.

BRENDA:

Certainly not a good sign, but it's important, Ted, that we don't jump to any conclusions here. She may just be in a situation where she can no longer transmit.

TED:

That's true Brenda. While we wait, let's recap what has happened so far for those that might be just joining us.

The anchors continued to chit-chat and stall while Steve Sampson desperately typed away, trying to reestablish a connection with his daughter. Russ Donovan, on the leading edge of a story he felt would take his news team to the top, wasn't about to let it go. The anchors were struggling, but he did not want to leave the story and switch to something else, risking another station scooping them on

breaking details. He twisted his mustache hard between his

fingers. Action, that's what he knew best. He had his ace

reporter, Rob Quick, at the cruise terminal ready to go live

with man-on-the-street reactions. He had sent Deanna

Portner to work on an OAR background piece, and Red

Chilton headed out to cover the economic impact of the

OAR Company on the Tampa Bay area. He dispatched

consumer reporter, Stan Ovello, to check out complaints

about OAR and to locate disgruntled former passengers.

Donovan's troops crawled the streets, owning the story.

He wondered how much of this enthusiasm and drive

stemmed from an incident three years ago when an

assignment editor had gotten a call that a small plane was

down off the Tampa Bay shoreline. Donovan, having been

with the station for a number of years in a lesser capacity,

had just landed the job of News Director. He yearned to

show his bosses they'd made the right decision. Just a hair

too slow on the draw, he sat waiting a crucial ten minutes

for confirmation that a small plane had, indeed, crashed. He

neglected to look further. When WTAM went on the air with

the story about a "small plane," other stations confirmed

that a 747 had crashed on approach to Tampa International

Airport. Donovan's crews sought a small plane in the water,

other stations ignored the little disaster and mobbed the

airport, shooting miles of video — a jet liner exploding on

the tarmac. Granted, being behind on a story happens every

day and television is so instantaneous that newsrooms can

cover their error and catch up quickly. But what happened

next tarnished WTAM's credibility for a good while.

A rookie reporter, Brad Kennedy, got to the airport

and jumped on the air, live, about to set off a chain of events

that would forever be known around the station as *the*

Kennedy Assassination. Intercepting people arriving in the terminal from parking areas and cab lines, he figured he had

the scoop on those coming in to pick up passengers from the

ill-fated flight. He grabbed elbow after elbow and tossed

rapid-fire questions.

"Did you know any of the passengers on flight 814

arriving from Detroit?"

"Yes, I'm here to pick up my wife and daughter," one

man finally told him.

"How do you feel, knowing no one survived the

crash?"

Kennedy, head up his behind and unaware of his

overwhelming aggressiveness, pictured himself doing a

stellar job catching live reaction to a tragedy. He continued

to pepper the stunned man with questions.

"What were your wife and daughter's names? Did

you get a chance to say goodbye? Do you wish they were on

another flight? Why weren't you on the flight with them?"

The seasoned camera operator couldn't stomach another minute and panned away from the man's tortured face, while Kennedy frantically motioned for him to pan back. In the studio, Donovan, impotent and beside himself with frustration, ran into the control room and barked orders.

"Commercial. Cut to commercial. Now!"

Too late. The damage was done. Kennedy, greener than mistletoe at Christmas, had managed to snag a war hero just returned from his second tour in Iraq. The rookie made the hero look like a careless husband that let his wife and daughter fly all alone and didn't even know when they were arriving. Sidebar: Kennedy had effectively notified the *last* of kin, the war hero, on network TV that his wife and only child were dead.

At a point, the City of Tampa's numbness over more than one-hundred deaths began to wane, and at the same point, anger over WTAM's callous unconcern for a war hero, and for human suffering, grew. Local newspaper editorials, exploiting their competition's bad fortune, called for the heads of everyone at the television station, from mailroom kids to Donovan and beyond. Angry callers lit up talk radio boards and phone lines.

"I don't know about you," one caller said, "but I'm sick of stupid, unfeeling reporters sticking microphones in people's faces when their family dies. You won't catch me tuning in WTAM any time soon."

Donovan sank lower into depression with each rabid radio diatribe. Their grammar and syntax might leave much to be desired, these vigilante callers, but their message was hitting loud and clear. Donovan fired the reporter, then decided the photographer, though he had tried to end the carnage, had to go, too. He even suspended himself for a week, taking the blame for letting a wet-behind-the-ears reporter go off unsupervised and undirected. He promised anyone who would listen that WTAM would do everything in its power to regain the people's trust. Still, news ratings plummeted to record lows, some nights so low that community affairs programs on the local college station had more viewers than did Donovan's half hours.

Time passed, as it always does, but Donovan spent the better part of two and a half years working to reverse the community's bad feelings toward his station. This day, he stood in the control room, watching a monitor. This day would be different. His ace reporter, Rob Quick, flickered on the screen, readying himself and his crew to go live from the cruise terminal. Donovan put his finger on the lever that put his voice into his reporter's ear.

He spoke hypnotically, softly, "Remember the Kennedy Assassination," he said. "Remember the Kennedy

Assassination." Then Donovan turned to check on Ted and Brenda.

TED:

Brenda, I'm told we are going to our reporter, Rob Quick, out at the cruise ship terminal getting reaction to today's events. Rob, what's the mood right now at the terminal?

ROB:

Well, Ted and Brenda, I can tell you it's not good. I've talked to several people that weren't sure if they would go on cruises they currently have planned. With me now is Peter Ginnamin, with his wife and young family. They have a cruise booked leaving this terminal tomorrow morning. Mr. Ginnamin, are you worried about leaving right now, based on what is allegedly happening in the Caribbean?

PETER:

Yeah, we really are. We're just not sure what we want to do.

ROB:

Will you ask for your money back?

PETER:

That's a real possibility. We're going to have to see what happens here in the next few hours. If the cruise line can assure me of my family's safety, then I guess we're going. But if not, we'll be looking for a refund. There's always Disney World!

ROB:

Thank you, sir. Well, Ted and Brenda, as you can see, the mood here is not good for future cruises. People seem pretty scared. There might soon be a line of vacationers asking for their money back.

In the OAR offices, after watching that interview, James Billington III crashed his fist onto the conference table, an atypical show of emotion and loss of controlled facade for him. "These idiots are planting ideas into people's heads. Where's Avery? She needs to get on the air and calm this situation down. Aren't we doing damage control, for the love of God?"

"Alright James, let's not lose our heads," Fen Jacobs soothed, taking a bit of guilty pleasure in his boss's loss of composure. "Maybe you should think about going on TV and calming this down, yourself. The people — our customers — trust *you*; they know *you* and probably want to hear from *you* at this point. Don't you think?"

Billington dissembled. "I'm a little busy right now trying to save my company," he said. "Anyway, it's her damn job, not mine."

"But if you go out there and talk, maybe that will help save the company, James," added Reid Klein. "Let's relax a bit — take a step back. This is an isolated event, not a trend. People might be scared away for a while, but they'll come back. We deal with the crisis, and we get back to normal. The sooner, the better."

Avery Jentelle re-entered the room, surveyed the crowd, and asked, ""Do we have updates? New information?" She ignored the icy glares. "Come on, does anybody know anything? Have we heard back from the pirates?"

"We know just what you know." Reid's tone dripped sarcasm as he amended, "We know whatever we've seen on TV."

"How do we have a billion dollar ship and no way to contact it?" Avery wanted to know. "As distasteful as it sounds, we've got to get in bed with these people if we want information," she added, pointing to the news anchors still verbally tap dancing on the television screen.

"I think you already are," came the typical Breslow goading.

"They're out to screw us, anyway," said Billington wryly. "I wouldn't share my gonorrhea with them."

"Hey, hold on a second," Reid said, standing up like he'd been hit by a bolt of lightning. "WTAM has the only information source coming out of the ship, right?" He didn't wait for a response. "But they don't know that *we* don't have a source, correct?" He looked around at the others in the room like a mad scientist. "Let's make up our own source. A source that's texting us, talking about how heroic our security department is, how our officers are dealing with the crisis. Let's hear how they've done nothing but take care of passengers above all else. It's pre-damage-control damage control."

Breslow nodded enthusiastic agreement, seeing his security people's reputation salvaged. Avery, shaking her head back and forth, protested.

"Will you listen to yourself? It's ridiculous. What if someone can prove later that our reports were lies? They'll crucify us, you know that. We can't control what's happening now, I admit. But I can spin it any way we like later. I can probably make it look like we staged the whole damn thing as an exercise."

"Cause that's just how good you are," Breslow intoned, chin cupped in his hands, elbows leaning heavily on the polished surface, eyeballs rolling like a teenager who's heard just about enough. All that was missing was a heavy uttering of *yeah, what evah*.

Avery, ignoring his sulks, continued, "Remember, this is the same television station that had zero credibility in this town after the plane crash incident a couple of years ago. People don't hang on their every word, as far as I can see. We're pitting the solemn word of media darling *James Billington III* — one of the most trusted men in America — against a television station already lacking in credibility and reach to some extent."

"Get serious, Avery, you can't possibly spin the dead people as actors in your scenario," sighed Jacobs. "I don't want anything to do with this anymore. I'm out." He exited the room after a parting remark, "Let me know if you need money authorized. Otherwise, I'm washing my hands of this fiasco."

Against a heavy silence, Billington began to speak, "Okay, I believe a compromise is in order here. I'll go on television. I'll tell them that, with our satellites down, there is no way they could be receiving messages from the girl or anyone else. As far as we're concerned, the messages are a fraud — the TV station has been had. They'll spend hours scrambling to pick up the pieces. Meanwhile, we can hope

the Air Force, or Marines, or Navy Seals, or whatever-the-

hell-else our government deploys in these situations will

have blown these pirate bastards to smithereens. After I do

that, Miss Jentelle, you will take the stage and figure out

something clever to say that will save our collective ass."

Avery, delighted with an action plan, grabbed

Billington's arm and ushered him down the stairs toward

the waiting television trucks.

CHAPTER FIFTY-TWO

Amina, having pulled her knife, crouched near Jen, cutting the girl's bonds as Captain Gunnar thrust the door open and rushed in. In full sprint, he met Amina's eyes. Though Amina had committed in her heart to jumping sides, she knew how this looked — like she was about to take Jennifer's life. Jen screamed, "Captain! *Stop!*"

But Gunnar, finished with wishy-washy hesitations, charged full speed and dove full body force into Amina's outstretched arm, her hand clutching the knife. He rolled over the top of her, and the knife sliced deep into his stomach. Amina careened back against the glass. Gunnar rolled away and turned over, making a half-attempt to stand.

The bloody knife lay on the floor between them. With great effort, Captain Gunnar shifted his eyes from the weapon covered in his blood, to his intestines spilling onto the floor. He didn't understand what he saw, and he felt the strongest desire he'd ever had to stand up and fight. As the extent of his injuries dawned on him and he recognized his plight, he knew he'd lose whether he stood or just lay there growing weaker, so he hauled himself to his feet. Wobbling, he lurched toward Amina, and the look on his face told her he would kill her. Amina dove for the knife. As she touched its slick, bloody surface, a powerful blow crushed into the side of her face. Gunnar hadn't conjured up the strength, and he moved his eyes again, taking in Jen's murderous face and still raised foot. He oozed to his knees then, and what was left of his body slumped to the ground, twitching and convulsing until he rasped his last breath.

Pissed now, Jen had had enough of adult messes, pirates, fear, and intimidation. People were dying all around her — *how is that ok?* She wondered, then decided it wasn't ok; it made her feel powerless and vulnerable. She moved toward the still shocked Amina and straddled her back.

Looking thoughtful and focused, Jennifer lifted the pirate

woman by the hair. Jen placed her left arm just underneath

Amina's jaw. She drew her right arm tight across Amina's

forehead, as though she were patterning studied, specific

moves. With the same violent motion that Cullen Nickels

had employed a few days before, young Jennifer Sampson

snapped Amina's neck. Surprised at how easy it felt, Jennifer

allowed the body to go limp and slump to the floor. She

studied the body for a moment and enjoyed the rush of

power radiating from her hands through her whole self. Jen

smiled just a tiny smile, hesitant, but satisfied. As she turned

away she spoke out loud, "One."

Through the window, Jen saw Dalmar and Erasto

walking the pilot to the helicopter.

For a moment, Dalmar couldn't figure his next move

and he wondered how this would play back home. The

other pirates, whose awe he coveted, would see him as a failure. A screw-up. He had gotten almost all his men killed, and he would crawl back with nothing to show. Could he make them believe he'd been successful? Nurturing that thought and hatching a new plot to make himself famous, he turned and fired three quick shots into Erasto's head. Dalmar poked the gun into the pilot's back and motioned for her to get aboard her chopper. In a trance, she fired up the blades and prepared for takeoff. Dalmar would go as far as he could with her, and he had no doubt of his ability to survive whatever lay beyond that.

While the chopper disappeared from view, Jen calmly picked her phone up off the floor and typed a message to her father.

I'm not scared anymore. I'm alright! Captain Gunnar saved my life and killed another terrorist to do it.

The control room at WTAM erupted with cheers as Steve read the text.

The Captain is dead. Don't know what happened to Mr. Nickels. I just watched the lead terrorist leave the ship on a helicopter. I think he may have been the only one left. We won, Daddy.

A second roar went up in the control room of WTAM when that message was received and instantly broadcast across the airwaves. The anchors, about to introduce a live interview with James Billington III, relayed directly to him that the crisis appeared to be over. Instead of being on the hot seat, Billington gushed about the Captain's heroism and his dedicated, well-trained crew. He promised that, whatever the cost, security would be forever tightened on his ships. He praised the efforts of passengers. He set his gaze squarely into the camera, his best side slightly tilted to catch the light, and vowed to do whatever it took to bring justice to those behind the attack.

"Make no mistake," he said authoritatively, sincerity framing every strong word, "those who did this will be punished. Our passengers, our brave crew, and the families of those killed or injured will be taken care of. We protect our own."

Avery Jentelle smiled broadly as she watched the screens in her office.

CEO Reid Klein and CFO Fen Jacobs sat silently in Reid's office, eyes on Billington's television presence. Billington was slick and loveable to the entire world, except for the two of them. They had hated his Teflon image for so long, and now they cringed as he, once again, slipped away squeaky clean. America's favorite executive did it again, but this time his execs had the last laugh.

Fen had first come up with his plan when he had sailed aboard one of the company's ships. He couldn't believe how approachable and easy-to-board those vessels were, especially when anchored off OAR Cay. Security was lax. Fen, on the shuttle, had struck up a conversation with an intelligent young man whose father owned the shuttle boats. The first thing that drew Fen to Ani Azar was the young man's tee shirt promoting the soccer World Cup. Fen was a big fan. The two talked for a while and Fen listened sympathetically to the tale of Ani's family's business being dumped by OAR. They realized they had a common enemy — James Billington III.

As far as Ani was concerned, *Billington* shut his father's business down without so much as a chance for them to captain the new shuttles. Ani's friend, Korfa Osman, happened to be well acquainted with the pirate, Abdi Dalmar. Osman just happened to convince Dalmar to abandon the familiar Arabian Sea for the unfamiliar

Caribbean. Ani later laughed at this crazy proof that

coincidence *does* happen.

The long and short of it, Fen and Reid were Teflon-

coated, too. They may not have ruined the reputation of

James Billington III and of OAR, his pride and delight, but

they stood on the edge of quietly collecting fifty million

dollars that had already been allocated.

Still in her office much later, Avery basked in the

relief of yet another PR disaster averted and she knew all

details would fall into place. She yawned, turned out the

lights, and left her office, stretching her neck as she rode the

elevator down to the street level. The drive home was quick

and uneventful, not surprising at midnight. At home, she let

herself in the front door, mounted the stairs, and walked

into her bedroom. Sitting on the edge of her bed, she pulled

off earrings, then shoes, wriggling her toes to get the blood circulating. Avery slid her stockings off and unbuttoned her silk blouse. She closed her eyes tightly, as much to relax them as to play back events of her day. Over her shoulder, she spoke to her husband already in the bed, but not asleep, "Long day," she said, simply.

Her spouse twirled his Fu-Manchu mustache between his fingers and lifted his large frame from the bed. He rubbed her shoulders and said wryly, "I know the rule is we don't discuss work at home, but how was *your* day?"

****

Resigned to his situation, Ani Azar stood on the empty deck of his shuttle and watched the evac helicopter carry Dalmar away. He turned and saw several military-looking copters approaching from the other side. He noticed a couple bags of Dalmar's wrist ties under a cushion, hatched a brilliant idea, and took the bag out of its hiding place. He arranged it on the cushion, placed his wrists on top of it, and secured it, using his teeth. He slammed his head into the bulkhead, knocking himself backwards and drawing a line of blood from his head to his jaw. Ani stood up woozily and forced himself to fall forward into the water. When he bobbed up, he found himself face-to-face with a bloating, floating corpse. *This,* he thought, *is a whole lot safer than being identified as one of the pirates.*

Chill, standing on his own boat, observed as Ani made his strange arrangements for survival. Chill, too, decided to act. He leaped into the water and struck out toward shore. The closer he got to shore, the larger grew the collection of people watching his approach from the beach. When he was about twenty feet out, several passengers waded into the water. *Ah, help,* he thought, happy with this outcome.

Rescuers reached his side and calm relief washed over his spent body, right before the rescue party beat the living hell out of him. Finally, when Chill wondered if he was done for, the largest member of the beach lynching squad sat on the suspected pirate and pushed his face into the ground until he coughed blood and sand. Soldiers, spilling from the chopper that had just landed, hustled toward the scene. More than one passenger could be heard taking credit for capturing a terrorist.

Above, in the sky, Cullen Nickels continued to bide his time under a blanket in the back seat of the helicopter. He had ample opportunity to consider his current state of affairs. His dear wife, who had known his darkest secret all along, had not forsaken him. But she was gone now. Could he go on without her? Anything could happen on this chopper, he knew. Maybe he'd be a hero if somebody bought the idea of him as an ordinary passenger assisting in a crisis. Of course, there was the little matter of pictures Jen had taken of him performing his *other* service. *Where the hell were those photos?* When the chopper banked away from the ship with its pilot and one other passenger; Cullen decided he had a last service to perform.

Cullen Nickels, ordinary passenger, emerged from under the blanket and wrapped his belt around the sturdy neck of Abdi Dalmar. *Fifty-four.*

The helicopter was a shape in the puffy white clouds when Jen emerged from the bridge enclosure, treasuring the fresh air and sunshine. She lifted her face to the warmth, then watched the helicopter rotor away and disappear into the sky. Hands in her pockets, she found and fingered the necklace she had swiped. What a long time ago that all seemed, and how silly for such a fuss to be made. She brushed wisps of unruly hair off her brow and decided she'd better head down and find her mom and brother. Descending the stairs for the umpteenth time that day, she hesitated. Looking hard and long at her cell phone, Jen became aware that she held the ability to destroy Cullen

Nickels. Hypnotized by the power and the choice she could

make, she stared into her phone's unwinking eye as though

some answer would text itself to her. Jennifer looked up,

thinking of how much she had learned about herself this

summer. She walked to the railing and dropped the cell

phone into the waiting sea.

EPILOGUE

Six months later.

Jen looked over the slew of college entrance papers that were assembled on the table in front of her. She wanted to be a Florida Gator, but at this point she was willing to go anywhere to get away from her permanently depressed mother and her deteriorating home life. After returning from the vacation from hell she had been hailed as a hero by the local media but she never felt as such.

She stared at the limp piece of pizza in front of her and thought about Robby and how he never got to have that last piece that he so desperately desired. His little body was unable to handle the surgery and when he made it home it was inside of the tiniest of boxed coffins. She pictured in her minds' eye his lifeless body inside the box and how he was probably wishing for a slice of pepperoni. She could see vividly his stillness inside his final confinement and it reminded her how fascinated she had always been by the

rhythm of breathing, and then by its cessation. She knew

then and there that whatever her life held in store for her

one thing was for certain; she had felt the ultimate thrill of

having your life on the line and surviving; and the even

more supreme power of taking life away. She liked the last

one better.....

To find out more about other works of Joseph Gaspare LoNigro, or to comment directly, you can visit him at www.joelonbooks.com